Alan Hunt
He left sch
father's farr ng on the
Norfolk Br the *Eastern*
Evening News. He also wrote poetry, some of which was
published while he was in the RAF during the Second
World War. By 1950, he was running his own book
shop in Norwich and in 1955, the first of what would
become a series of forty-six George Gently novels was
published. He died in 2005, aged eighty-two.

The Inspector George Gently series

Gently Through the Mill

Alan Hunter

ROBINSON

Constable & Robinson Ltd
3 The Lanchesters
162 Fulham Palace Road
London W6 9ER
www.constablerobinson.com

This paperback edition published by Robinson,
an imprint of Constable & Robinson Ltd, 2011

A copy of the British Library Cataloguing in
Publication Data is available from the British Library

ISBN: 978-1-84901-502-8

Typeset by TW Typesetting, Plymouth, Devon

Printed and bound in the EU

3 5 7 9 10 8 6 4 2

IN MEMORY OF *THUNDERBIRD*

A Broads gaff sloop in the classic tradition, 27ft 6in by 8ft 6in by 2ft 9in. Built at Wroxham in 1913 by Alfred Collins and christened *Windmill*, she has been a thing of beauty about the Broads for nearly a century. Few yachts of her class were faster or sweeter to handle, none could get their shoulders down and drive up into the wind with such power and vivacity. Now she is old, but long may she linger. She enriched the author by two *Thunderbird* summers.

CHAPTER ONE

WHY WAS THE baker in a temper that morning, shouting so loudly that one might hear him across the mill yard? It wasn't the way with Blythely, that quiet, chapel-going fisherman; nobody could remember the last time he had been in a temper.

'Didn't I tell you not to make a seed-cake mixture!'

It was Ted Jimpson, his young, fair-haired assistant, who was coming in for the full blast of it.

'We can't sell seed-cakes at Easter. How many more times have I got to tell you that?'

Sitting in his dusty little office by the mill gate, Fuller, the miller, could imagine the scene in the gloomy, sweating bakehouse. Poor, crestfallen Ted, his limp hair draped over his brow, was mumbling an excuse about the huge bowl of yellow mixture. Blythely would be standing by him, perspiration gleaming on his pale face.

'*I* said to make it up—!'

A pause while Ted offered his hesitant explanation.

'That's what *you* tell me. *I* don't remember it!'

1

So Blythely was being forgetful as well as in a temper.

Finally: 'All right – all right. We'll call it my mistake and put it in! But another time, young man—!'

Another time!

It was Blythely who had been wrong all along, and now he was too upset to admit it and apologize.

Across the yard the naphtha engine was thumping away in its pit, three small boys hanging round the open doors to watch the huge, half-buried fly-wheel. A big attraction to small boys was the rambling mill. They would love to have explored the many-floored mystery behind the dusty windows, the bridge which joined it to the bakehouse, the inexplicable hoists . . .

Fuller noticed Sam Blacker come out of the sack-store and make a threatening gesture towards the small boys.

'Clear out of it, you! Don't you know it's dangerous round here?'

The boys took to their heels, but stopped to jeer from a safe distance. Blacker waved his fist at them. Fuller, his lips compressed, turned to pick a letter from the pile his clerk had laid on the desk for him.

In the shop facing the street Blythely's wife was rushed off her feet by an impatient queue of customers. It was the only bakers in Lynton to open on Good Friday for the sale of hot cross buns, and what was more, they were the best buns in Lynton.

But Mrs Blythely didn't mind being rushed off her feet. She was a good-natured woman and she smiled at her customers as she handed over the white paper bags redolent of cinnamon.

'A dozen, Mrs Simmons? Your Ernie come home?'

She was popular with the customers. She was eight years younger than her reserved, straight-faced husband.

The town was awake and busy with people, though most of the shops were closed. Good Friday was an odd sort of day. You never knew who was working and who was not. The builders, for instance, and here at the mill . . . but other folk were dressed in their Sunday clothes, and some of them planning to attend the local league cup-final in the afternoon.

At seven in the evening there was to be a Procession of Witness led by the Vicar of St Margaret's. Heading the laity would be the mayor and mayoress, with such Lynton notables as the superintendent of police and Geoffrey Pershore, the affluent owner of the mill property.

The weather was going to be fine for it; Easter was late this year, and the pink blossoms of the ornamental cherries in the Abbey Gardens were already fluffing out.

'Hullo . . . is that Mr Brooks?'

Fuller was on the telephone to the grain warehouse by the docks.

'Look, Mr Brooks, I want that consignment of Canadian . . . yes, I know, but it's past ten and I haven't got a damned thing here to go on with!'

From the corner of his eye he could see the three small boys creeping back to the door of the engine-room.

'But don't your men work on Good Friday now?'

Each one was daring the other, their exaggerated stealth had something laughable about it.

3

'Well, I must have it this afternoon . . . two, at the very latest.'

Blacker flew out like an enraged ogre, scattering the three boys as a hawk scatters sparrows. They all dashed back down the narrow passage between the mill and the bakehouse. There, behind the mill, an old drying-ground formed a popular playground . . . why did the thought of it cause Harry Fuller to compress his lips again?

He hung up and swivelled round in his chair.

'Mary . . . get out a letter to Marshall's to say we'll be a day late delivering that consignment.'

'Shall I tell them why, Mr Fuller?'

'Naturally. Why should we take the blame?'

He got up and went out across the yard. Blythely was shouting again – how that man had lost his temper! In the sack-store Blacker was smoking a cigarette, and he didn't pretend to be doing anything else.

'Right – that Canadian stuff won't be here till this afternoon.'

Blacker shrugged. He was a tall, bony fellow with a humourless face and a weak mouth.

'We might as well pack up . . . have a holiday like other people.'

'I'll tell you when to pack up!'

Neither of them was looking at the other.

'That hopper of spoiled flour – now's the time to clear it out. Leave Tom and Sid to put the last of the oats through, and get the others on the hopper.'

He stalked out, not deigning to watch his order obeyed. Blacker was his new foreman, very new indeed was Blacker. Behind his back, Fuller knew, his employees were criticizing him for promoting such a fellow.

He stood by the mill gate and stared moodily across at the café opposite. To his left the shop bell tinkled prosperously as the customers pushed past each other.

'You got home all right last night?'

It was Bradshaw, secretary of the golf club, with whom he had been to a stag party which had lasted into the small hours.

'You must have been the only one who wasn't blotto . . . what did the little woman say, eh?'

Fuller managed to grin at him. His wife . . . as a matter of fact, she had never criticized him because of his annual binge. She was a very sensible woman. Though perhaps there was a limit to that.

He went back into the office and sat idle, listening to the thump of the naphtha engine. Behind him Mary was banging away at her typewriter, glancing at him now and then, no doubt, surprised at his inactivity. At thirty she was not unattractive. He was aware that she had no boyfriend and would probably accept a gesture from him.

'Are you doing anything for Easter, Mary?'

He half-turned, though without really facing her.

'Nothing much, Mr Fuller . . . I'm going on one of those coach trips to Blenheim Palace on the Monday.'

'Going with someone, are you?'

'Oh no, Mr Fuller. Just a little outing on my own.'

'Let me pay for the ticket. It'll be an Easter egg from the firm.'

Through her pleased expressions of gratitude he was thinking: 'Now if I'd been sensible, perhaps . . .'

There was a tap on the door and Fred Salmon, one of his hands, took a hesitating step into the office.

'Guv'nor . . .'

He was looking pale, even under the dusting of flour on his greyish features.

'What is it, Fred?'

'Guv'nor, you'd better come and see . . .'

Fuller stared at him a moment and then got quickly to his feet. It was plain from the man's appearance that something serious had occurred.

'An accident, is it?'

They were hurrying across the yard.

'I didn't like to say . . . his foot is sticking out of the sleeve.'

'Who? Who is it?'

'Christ knows, guv'nor. It isn't one of us.'

With a sickening feeling in his stomach Fuller bounded up the wooden steps to the sacking-room. It had happened once before, that, when he was serving his apprenticeship. A man had overbalanced and fallen into a hopper of flour. He remembered the terrible casualness of it. The man had simply disappeared into the expressionless white silence. Five minutes later, when they had managed to get a ladder down, the same man had been pulled out . . . soft, warm, but completely lifeless. For weeks he had been haunted by the horror of those five minutes.

They were standing round the sleeve, which had been

emptying into the wooden hopper-trolley. None of them seemed to know what to do, not even Blacker.

From the mouth of the sleeve protruded that single, terrible foot. It was wearing a cheap stamped-leather shoe and had completely obstructed the flow of sour-smelling flour.

'One of you . . . get some tools. You, Charlie – don't stand there gaping!'

Charlie Savage gulped and ran to go down the steps.

'Shut the flour off, one of you – Fred, get a ladder. We'll have to take the sleeve off. We'll never get him out the other way!'

He was in command, he was dispelling the panic, but the nausea in his stomach continued to grow. The precipice he had felt beginning to yawn at his feet that morning had suddenly opened wide below him. He had a strange impression of not being responsible for himself.

'Set the ladder against the beam. Sam, get in the trolley with Fred and take the weight of it.'

They went about his orders with a sort of plaintive eagerness, glad to make a show of normality in the business. 'Ease it down now – ease it! He can't be all that heavy.' Dead men were heavy, though. During the air-raids, he remembered . . .

Reverently they disencumbered the corpse of the canvas sleeve. The stiff foot persisted in sticking in the mouth of it, and Fred Salmon had to unlace the shoe, breathing through his teeth the while. Then they brushed the sour flour off it and laid it on the floor. It had stiffened in a crouched position and looked tiny and unnatural.

'Anybody know him?'

They made a pretence of studying the floury features. The man had died with a snarl on his face, showing the teeth like those of a beast.

But no, nobody knew him. In life and death he was a stranger.

'All right then – carry him down to the sack-store. I'll get on to the police and see what they make of him.'

Wordlessly they picked it up and went shuffling and clumsy towards the steps.

Fuller remained standing there, aware of the pallor showing beneath his eyes. And he was sweating, too, though it was a day with a chill breeze. Why . . . how? Why did he feel as though reality were slipping away from him? So some illicit prowler had taken a tumble into a flour-hopper!

He knew the police inspector who came to make enquiries. Griffin, his name was, and they had several times gone round the links together. But now there was a subtle change in the man. He was quieter, more watchful, he had no casual words to exchange.

'The mill buildings are locked, are they?'

'I always lock them myself.'

'Who would have the keys, sir?'

'I have, naturally . . . and Mr Blythely.'

'You wouldn't have noticed any forced entry, sir?'

'No . . . but there are plenty of windows with broken panes.'

There was nothing offensive about him, just a damnable persistence. He kept on asking questions long after a reasonable man would have left off.

'And you're sure you don't know him, sir?'

Three times he had asked that question.

'And you lock the mill buildings yourself?'

It was as though his mind couldn't grasp things and so you had endlessly to repeat them.

Fuller usually lunched at home, but today he felt unable to face his wife and the two younger children. On the phone he was cowardly and gave business as an excuse. In effect he joined Mary, who took her lunch across the road.

'A fine way to start Easter, Mary—!'

He wanted his voice to sound flippant, but he could hear the strained note in it. Neither could he fancy the food offered by the café.

'I've got that bad flour on my stomach . . .'

Only he knew it wasn't the flour.

Over in the shop, where the rush had long since ceased, he could see Blythely and his wife in a long and earnest conversation. On a bench in the mill yard Fred Salmon and Sid Neave sat eating their sandwiches and drinking cold tea.

It was more and more like a dream. He wondered how long it would be before he was unable to continue acting the part expected of him.

Mary, for instance . . . wasn't she already beginning to look at him a little queerly?

The inspector came back in the middle of the

afternoon. He had with him Geoffrey Pershore, the man who leased Fuller the mill, and a leading light in Lynton society. Pershore had a grave expression on his self-consequential features.

'Hullo, Fuller . . . could we have the office to ourselves?'

Mary took the hint and said she would go to fetch the tea. Pershore sat himself familiarly on the corner of Fuller's desk, taking care, however, to hitch up his finely creased trousers.

'This fellow you pulled out of the flour-hopper, Fuller . . .'

Fuller nodded automatically from the part of himself that was listening.

'I'm afraid it's more serious than it seemed. He didn't, it appears, die from suffocation in the flour.'

What ought he to do? How should he react?

'No,' continued Pershore, staring heavily at the varnished screen. 'According to the inspector, Fuller, that poor devil was strangled.'

The assistant commissioner was standing by his window when Gently tapped and entered. He might have been watching the courtyard or the segment of Embankment beyond, but Gently knew from experience that this was the A.C.'s way of chewing over a problem. He rustled the folder he was carrying and dropped it noisily into the in-tray. The assistant commissioner turned to survey him through heavy tortoiseshell-framed glasses.

'Ah, there you are, Gently. Is that the report on the Meyerstein business?'

Gently murmured inarticulately, never being one to waste his words.

'Well, take a pew there, will you?'

The assistant commissioner came slowly over from the window.

'There's a curious little matter which has turned up from the country . . . it's intriguing me a good deal, and I think it's right up your street.'

Gently sat as he was bid but with rather less than enthusiasm. Twenty years in the Central Office had taught him to be wary of cases which A.C.s found intriguing . . .

The assistant commissioner sat down also and took up an envelope which lay on his blotter. He shook out three photographs and pushed them across for inspection.

'Do you know these fellows?'

Gently nodded, spreading out the prints in front of him.

'They're a Stepney lot, aren't they . . . go around working the racetracks?'

'Mmn.' Gently nodded again. 'They've all got records. That's Punchy Ames, the rough-looking one . . . he's an ex-boxer who's been in for assault. The rat-faced one is Steinie Taylor . . . Roscoe, I think the other one is called.'

'Just so, Gently.' The assistant commissioner had removed his glasses and was dandling them in a distracting manner. 'And if you didn't find them in Stepney, where next would you look?'

'Well . . . any town with a racetrack, I suppose.'

'But if they weren't in Stepney and nowhere near a racetrack?'

Gently made a face. 'In stir – unless they'd cooked up a different racket for themselves!'

'Exactly.'

The assistant commissioner swung his glasses through a complete circle.

'And that looks like being the situation, Gently, as far as I can make out.'

He paused, making the glasses pause with him.

'You've seen the papers over the weekend?'

'Mmn . . . I glanced at them.'

'You noticed that curious affair at Lynton – the body being found in a flour-hopper?'

'It was all over the front page.'

'Well, then.' The glasses commenced to swing again. 'This is where we get the connection. Because the body in the hopper happened to belong to Steinie Taylor. The Borough Police have sent the prints up, and there's no possible doubt about it.'

Gently stared impassively at the three photographs on the desk. So that was the end of Steinie Taylor . . . ignoble, just as had been the man!

'What about the other two?'

The A.C. made a disclaiming wave.

'They disappeared from their haunts at the same time as Taylor, which as near as we can make out was a fortnight ago.'

'Have Lynton had their description?'

'Yes, but it doesn't seem to have helped them. They've got nowhere since Friday and now they want us to carry it.' Gently shrugged indifferently. It was the usual way of things. The locals tried their hand, and then passed the mess over to the Central Office.

'Killed about midnight Thursday, wasn't he?'

'That's the pathologist's estimate.'

'Much force used?'

'The usual fracture. Taylor was a little man.'

'Yes . . . I've had to do with him.'

The assistant commissioner twisted his glasses like a diviner's twig and appeared to be studying the set of them.

'You know what puzzles me – and it is a puzzle – is what the deuce those fellows were doing in a quiet little place like Lynton. What game were they up to? That's the star question. It was dangerous enough to get one of them murdered.'

Gently nodded agreement. 'Criminals work to a pattern.'

'There's that again . . . how did they get on to a different line?'

'It must have seemed worth the risk.'

'True – there'd be money in it. But what goes on at Lynton offering that sort of opening? And even if it did, how did they come to hear about it? There's your angle of attack for you, Gently. If you can find the racket I think you'll find your man.'

Gently grunted as he shuffled the photographs together. There was nobody like the A.C. for making the obvious sound inspiring.

At the same time he had been overlong in town, and a trip to the country was something he had been wishing himself.

'I'll have Dutt with me, will I?'

'Certainly, Gently. I know you make a good team.'

'He's working with Jessop just now.'

'I'll have him taken off directly.'

Gently went back to his office feeling that things might be worse in this second-best of all possible worlds.

CHAPTER TWO

I<small>T WAS TEATIME</small> at Lynton when the slow, stopping train from Liverpool Street eventually pulled in at the station. Over a cup of what the British Railways facetiously termed coffee Gently examined the evening paper and grunted his satisfaction. There was yet no mention of the Yard having been called in.

'We'll check in the cases and stroll across to look at the mill . . . it may give us some ideas to talk over with the locals.'

'Are we going to have a meal, sir, before we report?'

'I think so, Dutt. Not knowing their canteen.'

'I missed me lunch, sir, that's why I mention it . . . got shoved on this job in such a blinking hurry.'

Outside the station a grey road led them to the narrow streets of the town centre. At this hour they were thronged with workers returning from the big chemical works and other establishments on the town outskirts. Some afoot, many on cycles, they created an unwonted appearance of populousness, and the shops were busy with people making last-moment purchases.

A small town . . . what had three petty criminals found to do here which had ended in the death of one of them?

On a wide square a few brightly awninged stalls were selling off vegetables cheaply. In the distance the quarter chimed from the twin flint-faced towers of St Margaret's Church.

As they passed the Abbey Gardens they noticed a group of youths in drainpipe trousers lounging about the gates, opposite to them a few expensive cars parked in front of an old coaching inn called The Roebuck.

A bit of shop-breaking or rowdyism, that was the style of Lynton. If you got a murder here it would be an amateur job, somebody batting their wife and sticking their head in the gas oven . . .

'This is Fenway Road, sir.'

And over there would be the mill, an untidy yet somehow attractive jumble of buildings in a mixture of timber, brick and slate.

Gently came to a stop while he let the impression of it sink into his mind. It gave one the idea of irrational complexity, as though a simple idea had been carelessly embroidered upon.

At the front was the bakehouse and shop, a stark rectangular group in pinkish-yellow brick, three storeys high with the baker living over the shop. At the back it dropped a storey and became stores, outhouse, anything.

16

Behind this and nearly touching it rose the main block of the mill. It was quite a skyscraper, seven storeys at least. The brick here was dark red beneath blue-black tiles. The numerous square windows looked dusty and obscured, with sacks stuffed into frames which had lost their glass.

Much lower, but adjoining it, came a tiled and weatherboarded structure on a brick lower storey, and then a similar but higher erection with a shallow gable and an outside hoist.

A tall brick chimney sprouted from somewhere in the middle, a small office by the gate had low windows directly on to the road.

'A useful place to hide a body, sir!'

Dutt was also appraising it with a professional eye.

'I'll bet they don't use half of it . . . then look at all those outbuildings and things.'

'There's a yard or something at the back there, Dutt. You can see the tops of some trees over the roofs of those old cottages.'

'Our geezer was unlucky, wasn't he?'

'Yes . . . it might have been weeks before the corpse turned up.'

They moved along as far as the café, the sight of which provoked less professional thoughts in the mind of the hungry Dutt.

Some last few customers were being served in the shop by a talkative, fair-haired woman. In the office a middle-aged man with dark, bushy locks sat staring at some papers on his desk. As they watched a younger woman came through to him and her sudden appearance made him start perceptibly.

'Would that bloke be the miller?' muttered Dutt.

'It seems a fair bet.'

'Looks as though he's got something on his mind.'

'So would you have if you were on the wrong end of a homicide investigation . . .'

Gently sighed to himself and felt aimlessly about in the pockets of his raincoat. There was nothing suggestive here at all, nothing in the town, nothing in the mill.

Almost, he began to think, the whole circumstance was accidental . . . Steinie Taylor had got bumped off in some more promising venue, and his body was dumped at Lynton the more thoroughly to confuse the issue.

'Come on,' he said. 'Let's try this café before it closes.'

But Dutt was already turning the handle of the door.

Lynton Borough Police H.Q. had been burned down by incendiary bombs during the war and had since arisen, a tribute to contemporary style, from its literal ashes.

It stood facing the market square where it created no disharmony. The big, frameless windows, pastel brick, and supporting columns of varnished wood blended naturally with the Georgian setting, proving, if it were necessary, that good taste never quarrels with itself.

The super's office was in keeping with the architectural promise. It was lofty and light and discreetly furnished with chairs, desk, and filing cabinet in two-toned wood, while the carpet, by police-station standards, was unashamedly vivacious.

18

It had the smell of somewhere new: it smelled of linseed and dyed fabrics and fresh cement.

'Well, gentlemen, you know the outline of the case.'

Superintendent Press was sitting uneasily behind his desk, his hands moving restively as he talked to the Central Office men.

'This fellow Taylor and his associates are nothing to do with Lynton. I don't mind telling you that in our view the culprit will be found elsewhere.'

He was a man in his fifties with fleshy, boyish features. He had hard, greyish eyes and a fruity voice.

'Your people think it's a gang killing, and we have found nothing to suggest that it isn't. The obvious theory is that he was murdered by his associates. The fact that they have disappeared goes a long way to substantiate it.'

Gently nodded absent-mindedly and brought out his pipe. After looking round the town he was prepared to concede this theory as being the obvious one.

'As to what they were doing in Lynton, your guess is as good as mine. I understand that these three men were in the habit of frequenting racetracks, but there is nothing closer to Lynton than Newmarket and Lincoln. The last racing in the vicinity was at Newmarket three weeks ago.'

In the square below the window a man was feeding the pigeons. The red sky of a fine April evening outlined a satisfying horizon of Georgian roofs and chimneys.

'We've got another idea . . . we think it might be unconnected with racing.'

'Wouldn't that be unlikely?'

'Uncharacteristic, but then, so is murder.'

The super jiffled with even greater unease.

'What exactly did you have in mind – burglary, something of that sort?'

No.' Gently shook his head. 'That would be *too* uncharacteristic. Burglary is a specialist crime – you don't find other criminals casually turning to it. What we should look out for is some sort of a racket, something which has suddenly provided a special opportunity. We'll suppose that our three men heard about it and came to cash in . . . then they ran up against some opposition and one of them got killed. The other two, quite naturally, dropped the business like a hot brick.'

'And all this in Lynton?'

'We can't be quite certain.'

'You can be certain enough of that one thing, Inspector. There are no rackets being operated in Lynton.'

A big diesel truck crossed the square and sent the pigeons momentarily fluttering. The man who was feeding them threw his last fragment and crumpled the bag into a ball.

'You have some docks here, haven't you?'

Gently blew a quiet little smoke-ring.

'Yes . . . in a small way. Only light-draught vessels can come through the estuary.'

'Any continental traffic?'

'A few timber boats from Germany and Scandinavia.

20

There's a Dutch ship, I believe, which carries on a coal trade.'

'There might be something there.'

The super frowned at his fingernails.

'As a matter of fact we did have a case ... but no stretch of imagination could make a racket of it. Inspector Griffin, you handled that business. Perhaps you can give Chief Inspector Gently an account of it.'

Inspector Griffin sat up a little straighter. He was a lean, fit-looking man with a severe moustache and a severe manner.

'February the twenty-third, I think, sir. On information received I detained a German seaman named Grossmann as he was leaving the cargo-vessel *Mitzi*, arrived from Bremen with a cargo of machine-spares. He became violent and I was forced to restrain him. On being searched he was found to be carrying a package containing several thousand grains of heroin, and more was discovered in his sea-chest. We obtained a conviction, sir.'

'And that, I think, is our only serious case of smuggling, Inspector?'

'Yes, sir. For as long as I've been on the Force.'

The super extended an exonerated hand. 'You see? A single case involving a solitary individual.'

'Mmn.' Gently puffed steadily. 'And the person he was going to sell it to?'

'He'd got no contact, sir.'

Griffin came in like a bullet.

'He was a rather stupid and uneducated man with no knowledge of what he was doing. Apparently he was under the impression that he could sell heroin to the nearest chemist or doctor. It was obviously the first time he had attempted anything of the sort.'

Gently shrugged and struck himself a fresh light. At all events he was trying to get straw to make some bricks from . . .

'There's nothing else you can think of?'

He was looking towards the super, but his question was addressed to Griffin. The super, he felt, had present visions of a shining, crime-free Lynton.

'We have our quota of petty crime, but nothing at all out of the way.'

'No forgeries, defalcations, outbreaks of armed assault – that sort of thing?'

'Nothing of the sort has come to our notice lately.'

They were on the defensive, both of them. The super had a stubborn expression on his fleshy face and Griffin was intent, ready to throw up his guard.

You had only to suggest for one moment that there might be undiscovered crimes lurking in the district . . .

'Well, we'd better leave that angle and get down to brass tacks. Who have we got at the mill, and what have they got to say for themselves?'

Immediately the atmosphere relaxed. The super, opening a drawer, produced a box of cigarettes and offered them around, irrespective of rank. Inspector Griffin picked up a file he had brought with him and rustled the sheets in it with an air of confidence.

'First there's the people who live on the premises . . . Henry Thomas Blythely, the baker, and Clara Dorothy Blythely, his wife. And you have to count the assistant, Edward John Jimpson. He was working in the bake-house during the time the crime was committed.'

It had been a busy night, the one preceding Good Friday. Unlike his fellows Blythely baked the hot cross buns to be fresh on the day. The addition of these to his regular quota had meant an early start, and both his assistant and himself were in the bakehouse by ten p.m. on the Thursday evening.

'And that's their alibi – they worked right through together. At seven in the morning they knocked off for a couple of hours, Blythely taking a nap on his bed and Jimpson on a shake-down at the back of the shop. But the latest time the pathologist gives for the killing is two or three a.m.'

'And the earliest?' interrupted Gently.

'Ten or eleven p.m. on the previous evening.'

Nothing was known to the demerit of either Blythely or his assistant. The baker's wife, by her own account, had retired to bed soon after her husband had gone down to the bakehouse, and had been wakened by him at seven in order to open the shop at half past.

'Now we come to the mill people, though it seems unlikely that they would have had anything to do with it.'

First the miller, Harry Ernest Fuller. He had locked up the mill at six p.m. on the Thursday and gone home to have tea with his wife and two young children. It was the night of the annual stag party given by his golf club. He had arrived at this – it was held in a pavilion attached to The Spreadeagle public house – at eight p.m., and left it again at approximately three a.m. on the Friday morning, the time being vouched for by his wife and an employee at the establishment.

Griffin paused before he continued.

'This may be irrelevant, sir, but I think I ought to mention it. Fuller impressed me unfavourably in the way he answered my questions. I didn't attach much importance to it because the man had just had a bad shock, but I feel that the chief inspector ought to have all the facts.'

Gently nodded his compliments and puffed on at his pipe. It didn't take long to sum up Griffin as a conscientious officer. He'd lost his case, it had been given to the Yard, but that wouldn't stop him handing over what might be of assistance.

'There are a foreman and six hands employed at the mill, and two drivers who deliver and pick up grain.'

Griffin had questioned each one and checked on his story. No fish was too small for the C.I.D. man's painstaking net. This one had been in a pub, that one at the cinema. Blacker, the foreman, had had to admit a night with a woman of the town. But they were all accounted for, even Miss Playford, Fuller's clerk.

None of them could be truthfully described as suspects, and all of them had reasonable alibis.

'Any bad hats amongst them?'

It seemed that there were not. Blacker, perhaps, had

a taste for low company, but it had never run him into any cognizable trouble.

'Fuller for instance . . . has he got any money troubles?'

Another blank there – the miller was mildly prosperous.

The super was listening to it all with an expression of benignity. His man had done a good job and the rider was self-evident.

'I think you'll have to admit, Inspector, that Taylor's associates are your men. There's nobody here who even knew the fellow, let alone had a motive.'

Yes, it was getting plain enough. The more you listened, the more you probed, the less probable did it seem that Lynton had any more than a proprietary interest in the crime which had been fathered on it.

On the roof where they had retired the pigeons cooed their complacent innocence.

'Fuller and Blythely were the only ones with keys?'

'Yes, but several ground-floor windows are broken.'

'You checked them, of course?'

'I was unable to come to any definite conclusion.'

'Who knew that the hopper of sour flour might go undisturbed for a week or two?'

'Almost everyone . . . it was an odd job which would get done only when the routine work was held up.'

Back and forward went the shuttlecock, with Griffin never at a loss for his reply. He had thought of it all and checked it all; one could picture him going his rounds, quiet, alert and ruthlessly pertinacious. He had wanted the facts and he had got them; where Griffin had been, Scotland Yard must follow suit.

'And there's no trace of any of these three having stayed in the town?'

As the conference progressed Gently was hunching ever deeper into his comfortable chair.

'We've talked to all the lodging-houses and cheap hotels. A man disappeared on that date from one address, but we managed to trace him and he was only bilking his landlady.'

'What about the other hotels?'

'Would these men be likely to stay in them?'

'Not in the usual way, but it's just possible that they were in the money.'

Griffin hesitated and for once looked put out. But he quickly recovered his stride.

'We are always informed, of course, if anything irregular has occurred. Nobody could disappear from a hotel in the town without us hearing about it.'

'His pals might have paid his bill.'

Griffin looked as though he thought it were unlikely. Gently thought so too, but he lingered over the point. It was the only time he had caught the efficient inspector napping . . .

Outside the shadows were lengthening in the square. A few knots of people had emerged from the Corn Exchange, where a concert was in progress. They were spending the interval talking and smoking cigarettes.

'Well, I suppose that covers the case in outline.'

Relief showed in Griffin's face, and the super could not repress an audible sigh.

'If you'll let me have the reports I'll go through them this evening. Tomorrow, perhaps, we can do a little checking.'

They rose and shook hands, the super now cordial in his expressions of goodwill and offers of cooperation. A car would be at their disposal, an office was set aside for them. The super personally had booked them rooms at the St George Hotel, which they could see across the square.

Gently thanked him and left clutching Griffin's well-stuffed file. Dutt tagged along behind him, a gloomy expression on his cockney features.

'They certainly pick them for us, don't they, sir?'

Gently grunted and tapped out his pipe on his heel.

'Everythink cut and dried – except they haven't got the leading suspects. So they calls us in to produce them out of a flipping hat.'

Gently pocketed his pipe and paused in the cobbled centre of the square. Such a quiet, quiet town! The bells of St Margaret's sounded like a complacent benediction, the pigeons had settled finally to roost on the tower of a little church.

It might have been an artist's picture of provincial peace and lawfulness.

'We'll check the hotels though . . . you can do it tomorrow. There's an outside chance of a lead on Ames and Roscoe.'

'Yessir. But if I don't find nothink?'

Gently shrugged. 'You know as well as I do. We're here to scrape the barrel. After that it's just a question of waiting for those two to turn up . . . it's difficult to hide for ever in a country as small as this.'

CHAPTER THREE

THE ST GEORGE Hotel was one of those modest paragons of innkeeping virtue which, where they occur, are usually played down and kept quiet about; it was unmistakably a good thing.

Another example of the coaching inn, it had an unimpressive plastered front no larger than the average public house. But when you went through into the courtyard you saw the extent of the four sides, and heard without surprise that there were forty rooms available.

Gently lingered at the desk as he and Dutt booked in.

'Did you have any guests who left hurriedly on Good Friday . . . they would probably have been here a fortnight or so?'

The receptionist, a dark, strong-faced woman, looked thoughtful and then shook her head.

'As you see from the book, sir, we had nobody leave over the weekend.'

'What about these people?'

He showed her the photographs.

'I can't be certain, but I don't think we've ever had them here.'

They had roast pork for supper and after it a liqueur brandy with a cigar. Gently leafed through Griffin's file while they sat in the lounge. It gave chapter and verse for everything the inspector had told him, but added nothing which struck one as being the least bit suggestive.

'All well – we'll sleep on it!'

That was often a good recipe. One's mind sometimes sorted things out during the dark hours.

They retired to spacious rooms with enormous sash windows, and beds so large that you hardly knew where to start on them. And after London, the quietness seemed almost uncanny.

The morning showed grey with a chilling east wind. Gently had ordered three papers and he had got a press notice in each of them. At breakfast he was warned that there were reporters waiting in the hall, and he put on his most wooden expression when he went down with Dutt.

'Are you expecting to make quick progress?'

'I can't say at this stage.'

'Do you think Ames and Roscoe are in Lynton?'

'We have no indication.'

'Taylor double-crossed them, did he?'

'On the facts the theory is feasible.'

They took some photographs which he knew would portray him villainously, and hastened away to catch the lunchtime editions.

'Phew!' Dutt scratched his head and made an expression of comical disgust. 'They aren't half keen on this one, sir – we're going to be in the flipping headlines.'

He despatched Dutt to Headquarters to get a list of the hotels and himself set off in the direction of the mill. It was Wednesday, one of the two market days, which brought an influx of country people. There were more stalls in the square than had been there on the previous evening.

In the Abbey Gardens the east wind was chopping off the cherry blossom, scattering it in drifts about the gravel walks. The dull sky made the town seem frigid and unfriendly. People went about with faces which were glum and set.

An exception was the mill itself, which somehow exerted an air of benevolence. It may have been the jolly thumping of the naphtha engine or the sweet, warm smell of grain; and then there were whiffs of new bread from the bakehouse, and the general disreputable appearance of the whole.

Gently tapped at the door of the office and entered.

The man with the dark bushy hair was standing at the door of the screen talking, but he broke off and closed it as his visitor came in.

'Can I do something for you?'

'I'd like to have a talk . . .'

'Oh – you're from the police, are you?'

'Chief Inspector Gently, C.I.D., Central Office.'

Griffin was right again, the man impressed one

unfavourably. A quick flush had come over his bold features and his brown eyes darted away uneasily.

He was not unhandsome; he was about fifty. Without being tall he looked muscular, his shoulders broad and a little rounded.

He had a tenor voice with a careless provincial accent.

'I heard they'd called the Yard in, but I thought they'd have finished with this side of it.'

'We always like to make our own check ... Mr Fuller, is it?'

'That's right – I'm the boss here.'

'I'd like you to show me round the mill, Mr Fuller. But first I wanted to have a private talk with you.'

'Mary!'

Fuller turned his head and jerked out the word. The rather pretty girl whom Gently had seen from the café came to the door of the screen.

'Mary, be a sport and fetch my *Mills and Milling* from the bookstall ... I'd have a tea break, too. I shan't be wanting you for half an hour.'

Mary took the hint and departed, not daring to throw a glance at Gently. Fuller watched her disappear round the corner before motioning Gently towards a chair.

'You've talked to Inspector Griffin, of course?'

Gently nodded and seated himself.

'Well, I don't know what else I can tell you, though I'll be happy to help all I can.'

He was putting a bold front on it, but a child could see that he was nervous. He was having to stop his mouth from twitching and his eyes moved restlessly from object to object. Instead of sitting he remained leaning awkwardly against the screen.

'With regard to keys, Mr Fuller . . .'

'They're with me and Mr Blythely – oh, and Mr Pershore, he could have a set.'

'You mean the owner of the property?'

'Yes – he might have some, don't you think?'

'Mmn.' Gently didn't sound impressed. 'But they wouldn't be strictly necessary?'

'Not to get into the mill. There's three or four busted windows . . . we've had kids roaming round there before. The engine-room needs a key, but that's about all, I reckon.'

'Isn't it rather tempting providence?'

'It's the same with every mill.'

'Do you close the gates, for instance?'

'There's no point in it. You can get in through the drying-ground at the back.'

So the mill had been wide open, beckoning to any passer-by. Late at night you could have run a car into the yard, provided Blythely didn't hear you from the bakehouse.

'You don't remember any strangers about the place?'

'I can't say I do.'

'It seems credible to you that a stranger could have got in and dumped that body in the hopper?'

'If they could get into the place what was to stop them dumping the body?'

Nothing, of course. Nothing at all. But why then was Fuller nervous? Was it just a natural reaction towards being questioned by a policeman, or was it something other and more interesting?

'They tell me you've got quite a good Midland League side at Lynton.'

Fuller's eyes found him quickly, alarmed at a question the drift of which he couldn't fathom.

'Yes, it's not bad. They won the East Counties Cup on Friday.'

'You didn't see the match, naturally.'

'How could I, with all this business going on? In any case, we work on Good Fridays.'

'You follow them, though, do you?'

'I suppose so, when I get the chance.'

'Do you have a flutter sometimes?'

'A flutter?'

Fuller could sense a danger which he was unable to identify.

'I don't bet a lot, if that's what you mean. Just a quid now and then on something I fancy.'

'You prefer to watch them, I expect.'

'I do, as a matter of fact.'

'Were you at Newmarket, for example, when they ran the Spring Handicap three weeks ago?'

'I – no – yes, yes, I was! But what the devil has that got to do with it?'

Gently shook his head indifferently. 'Nothing, I dare say. Unless you chanced to meet up with Taylor and his pals on the racetrack.'

Fuller didn't do what he expected, jumping in with protestations of innocence. Instead he remained quite silent, his flush deepening and his lips tightened to control their quivering.

The pounding of the engine across the yard seemed to be vibrating the whole universe.

'Would you believe me if I said I didn't?'

'Why not?' Gently shrugged. 'I've got no evidence.'

'I didn't, you know – I was there with my wife! She'll swear I was with her every damned minute.'

'Then I won't press the point.'

'But you don't believe me, do you?'

'It is immaterial for me to believe what I can't prove, Mr Fuller.'

Again he was expecting an outburst and again it failed to come. The miller relapsed into an angry silence and stood digging with his nail at a crack in the varnished screen. Outside, two men in dusty denim jackets went lurching across the yard with a coomb sack of grain between them.

'Can we go over your statement, perhaps?'

'It's been gone over – time and time again.'

'All the same, I'd like my personal impression.'

'I tell you they've had it all – Griffin's never stopped getting at me.'

'Wasn't it at six p.m. when you locked the mill up?'

There was something there, and Gently went after it pitilessly. Griffin had smelt it with his conscientious nostrils, and now Gently had caught the selfsame odour. It was unlikely but it was there – and in the first instance one simply took up the pursuit.

'What happened when you arrived at The Spread-eagle?'

'I had some beer and played a game of darts.'

'And after that?'

'We had our dinner. It went on till midnight. A lot of people made speeches – you know the sort of thing. A bit near the knuckle, and smuttier as they went on.'

'You were at table till midnight?'

'I won't swear to the hour.'

'You were not absent, I mean?'

'I – well, I may have gone to the toilet.'

After dinner the affair became a little more muddled. Almost everyone was drunk or well on the way. There had been more speeches and songs and somebody danced on a table-top. Two revellers passed out and several were being sick in the toilet.

'You didn't pass out, though?'

'No, but I was sick. We had lobster at dinner and it sometimes disagrees with me. I had to go out into the yard to retch and get some fresh air.'

'What time was this?'

'Oh – when we got up from dinner. It was all right when I was sitting but it hit me when I got up.'

'You were out there alone?'

'Is it usual to retch in pairs?'

'How long were you out there, Mr Fuller?'

'My God, you don't think I timed it! I was there half an hour, perhaps – longer, it might have been. When I came back in I had a glass of tonic water. If you don't believe me you'd better ask the waiter.'

'So it was approximately from twelve to half past, was it?'

'I said before that I couldn't swear to the time.'

'According to the proprietor the dinner was over by half past eleven. Would that mean that you were absent for an hour?'

'Nothing of the sort! It was half an hour at the most.'

'The Spreadeagle is only five minutes' walk from here.'

It was a chink, but a narrow one. Fuller could easily have got to the mill and back. But with only twenty minutes to spare – his account checked well with Griffin's findings – he would need to have been lucky to have murdered and disposed of Taylor.

'The waiter thinks it was later than midnight when he served you with the tonic water.'

'*I* didn't say it was midnight – that's what you tell me.'

'We know you went outside after the dinner, but not when you came back.'

'If the dinner ended at eleven thirty then I was back by midnight.'

Like Griffin, he found that the chink wouldn't open. He was getting all the same replies, and it was long odds that they were true.

Unless Fuller had a motive, what was the significance of opportunity? He might have been at Newmarket, but who could swear that Taylor had been there?

As for the vomit, Griffin had duly inspected the yard and noted some . . .

'You went home at three a.m., didn't you?'

'So the wife says. I went home when it broke up.'

'You walked, I believe?'

'In that condition I would hardly have driven.'

'There are taxis, Mr Fuller.'

'At that hour in Lynton it's simpler to walk.'

'Why did you empty the hopper the next morning?'

About that he talked freely. It had clearly no anxieties for him. Omitting nothing in the report, he described how the consignment of grain had been delayed, how he had put the men on the hopper, and how one of them, Fred Salmon, had fetched him out of the office.

'We thought it was an accident . . . a long time ago the same thing had happened. What we couldn't make out was who the bloke was and what he'd been doing in the mill.'

'Did anyone act queerly?'

'We didn't none of us think much of it. There were a few pale gills about, but what were you going to expect?'

Just that of course, and no other. The phrase summed it up consummately. One saw the silent group of mill workers standing near their grim discovery, the un-reckoned danger of the flour-hoppers brought suddenly and unanswerably home to them.

But for the grace of God . . .

'What did they say?'

'It was me who did the talking.'

'You're sure nobody recognized him?'

'I asked them and that's what they told me.'

'What happened then?'

'I had him put in the sack-store out of the way. Then I phoned the police and sat trying to figure out what he'd been after in the mill. The men knocked off for a cup of tea. I didn't find them another job until they came back after lunch.'

Now Fuller seemed uneasy again, though heavens knew why he should be. As though the straightforward discovery of the body was a little island of blame-free certitude in an anxious sea.

'I still thought it was an accident, of course. It wasn't till later they came in . . .'

'It must have been a grave shock, Mr Fuller.'

The brown eyes jumped up to him. 'Yes . . . but in a way . . .'

They remained looking at each other for a long moment, the miller unable to disengage from the treacherous rapport he had established.

'You understand . . . I'd been thinking! There are two ways, and naturally . . .'

'You mean that you suspected foul play?'

'No! But it was so odd, his being there. We didn't know him, we'd never seen him . . . his clothes and everything. It simply wasn't natural. I couldn't help feeling . . .'

Gently held his eyes mercilessly and let him stumble on.

'It was a premonition, don't you see? I suddenly felt I was in . . . no, not that . . . but it was going to make trouble. Mr Pershore wouldn't like it, you see? He hates any scandal! And then the reputation . . . wouldn't do the business any good. Altogether I had an idea . . . you understand me?'

He faltered to a stop, and Gently hunched a careless shoulder. So it hadn't been a shock to Fuller when he had heard that Taylor was murdered! But then, who wouldn't have thought about it and had his premonitions? Good Friday, as a matter of interest, had occurred on the thirteenth.

'You were right, weren't you? It's made a bit of trouble.'

Fuller nodded in relief. 'Yes . . . that's what I was trying to say.'

'Everyone was suspect even though they were in the clear.'

'God, yes! That's the feeling. And I could sense it coming on.'

'But you had seen nothing to substantiate that feeling?'

'No, not a thing.'

'You didn't know Taylor and you've never met any of these people?'

Gently displayed half a dozen photographs among which were those of Ames and Roscoe.

Fuller examined them and shook his head.

'I don't know any of them from Adam.'

'Then that's all for the moment. But now I should like to see over the mill.'

There was no help for it, he was plodding in Griffin's footsteps. He hadn't got an inch further than the Lynton man's report. Fuller had roused both their interests only to lull them both to sleep again. He impressed one unfavourably, but on the balance one could attach no importance to it.

'That's the sack-store in there if you want to take a look at it.'

The surface of the mill yard was uneven and broken by decades of lorries. A dozen plump pigeons ran on it – Lynton was a great place for pigeons.

'The engine-room doesn't connect with anywhere. As I told you, we keep it locked.'

An elderly man in oil-stained dungarees came to the door, wiping his hands. Behind him the huge fly-wheel quivered as it spun. A smaller wheel drove the strap which connected to some overhead shafting. A twirling governor kept the whole amazing contraption in order.

'The kids come and look at it – they take a short cut through the drying-ground. If you go down the passage there you'll see what I mean.'

The passage was the division between the biggest mill building and the bakehouse block. The layout was a rough square of which the passage opened an inside corner.

Between the two blocks ran a narrow bridge at first-floor level, beneath which was one of the doors to the mill.

'Does Mr Blythely have the key of the door across the bridge?'

'That's right, we both have one. I use the back of his place as a store. The blokes keep their bikes in the room underneath – Inspector Griffin went over it, but I don't think he found anything.'

He didn't, it was in his report. He had ransacked the entire premises and found nothing except flour dust.

'What's this drying-ground you talk about?'

'Keep going and you'll come to it.'

The passage turned a corner and then ended in an open space hemmed in by a high wall and the backs of uninhabited cottages. It was about sixty yards by fifty, part cinder, part grass, with two or three overgrown pear trees grouped at one spot. A few old posts for drying-lines still formed a triangle in the middle. At the corner against the bakehouse stood a dilapidated stable with a hayloft over it.

'There's a blasted right-of-way through here . . . you come in from Cosford Street by that other passage in the far corner. It's not a short cut at all, but the kids always use it. And of course they make this a playground . . . that's how our windows get broken.'

'It looks ideal for kids.'

'They're into everywhere.'

'Is that stable in use or is it just falling down?'

Fuller looked at it frowningly. 'It belongs to Blythely . . . he hasn't used it for years. I keep some hay in the loft to sell to odd customers.'

'And the kids romp in there?'

'Yes – I suppose so.'

Gently's eyebrow lifted imperceptibly at the abruptness in the other's tone. Fuller looked discomposed and was feeling for a cigarette.

'Of course, neither of you keeps a horse . . . ?'

'Not since Blythely bought a van – and that was before the war.'

With a sort of violence Fuller crossed to the stable and

threw open the doors. Inside was a collection of rubbish which plainly precluded recent equine occupation. The horse-collars and harness hanging from pegs were gaping and perished with age.

'No horses – you see?'

Gently nodded gravely.

'I watch them and bet on them, but I was never fool enough to own one . . . now if it's all the same to you, I'd like to get on with showing you the mill.'

Gently followed him back into the passage and through the door beneath the bridge. Inside the smell of grain and flour was so strong as to be almost overpowering.

'It's just shafting down here – watch yourself as you go under! On the next floor are the rollers, then the purifiers. The bolters are right at the top.'

All the building was a-shudder with the thud of the engine. Hidden machinery murmured and rumbled about them. On a wide wooden floor, polished smooth by the passage of grain, lay a spreading pile of reddish wheat; two men with wooden shovels were feeding it into a shute.

'This stuff's Canadian.'

Fuller was having to raise his voice.

'We mix it with the English to get a proper blend. People talk about the home-grown product, but they'd soon complain if they got it unblended.'

They kept going up by means of heavy wooden steps. It was not until the third floor that they came to the open mouths of the flour-hoppers. Four in line, protected by a single wooden rail, they descended like tapering wells to the sacking-room on the first floor.

One of them was full, one of them half-full. For a moment the snowy contents amazed one with their innocence . . .

'Drop anything in there and it simply keeps going. It's not like water. There's no support at all.'

'Which one did you find him in?'

'That one at the end. Some diseased grain had gone through, and it turned the whole hopper foisty – we were busy at the time, so I left it just then.'

'Wouldn't you say the person who dropped him in there had some idea about mills?'

Fuller flushed as he said: 'He knew where to find the hoppers, didn't he?'

They went down past the rolling machinery to the sacking-room with its dust-hazy atmosphere. Here the mouths of the hoppers, each provided with a damper, were extended by sleeves of canvas to a convenient level. Four men were filling sacks from the two charged hoppers. A fifth, a tallish, heavily boned fellow, was leaning against an upright and smoking a cigarette.

'This is Blacker, my foreman.'

Fuller scowled at the cigarette.

'This is Chief Inspector Gently of the Yard, Blacker. He's in charge of the case now, so you'll no doubt be seeing more of him.'

Blacker eased himself off the upright and slowly stubbed out his cigarette. He had a long, humourless face with green-grey eyes, a wide, weak mouth and stick-out ears. When he spoke his voice sounded harsh and clumsy.

'I thought they'd finished with us . . .'

'Well, they haven't, it seems.'

'Shouldn't think there's much left here to find out.'

'Let's hope there isn't. We've had enough trouble.'

What was it between them, the master and his foreman? Gently sensed it directly, that slight, fraying edginess.

Blacker stared at him insolently as though he were some odd exhibit. The fellow had an expression of cunning mixed with derision in his eyes. He kept his cigarette in his hand, ready to light it when their backs were turned.

'I want the whole of this lot sacked up before lunch.'

'Daresay you'll get it if we aren't held up.'

'After lunch you can start putting the oats through.'

'So you told me when I came in.'

Fuller turned on his heel and went down the steps into the yard. The pigeons, scattered for a moment, settled again with a soft music of wings.

At the bakehouse door a blond-haired youngster in a white apron was filling a bucket from a tap. He looked up curiously as the miller went by with Gently.

'Your foreman been with you long?'

'Yes . . . no, not as a foreman, that is.'

'You mean you've just made him up?'

'Yes, I suppose so. Though it was probably a mistake.'

'When would he have been appointed, Mr Fuller?'

The miller made a gesture of exasperation. 'Does it

really matter? I gave him the job on Good Friday. Some time or other I'd like to forget that day!'

Gently nodded his mandarin nod and fumbled for his pipe. Fuller was standing by grimly with his hand on the door to the office.

'One point more . . . touching those hoppers. Did any of the others have flour in them on Thursday night?'

'Number one at this end had flour in.'

'That's the one nearest the steps?'

'Yes. It was three-quarters full.'

'Thank you for being so helpful, Mr Fuller.'

The miller banged into his office, letting the door slam behind him. The pigeons made to rise again but then thought better of it. Each one, nevertheless, kept a bright eye fixed on Gently.

CHAPTER FOUR

FROM SOMEWHERE, EVERYWHERE it seemed, came the chirrup of a cricket. It was as though the moist, savoury heat were making itself audible. At the same time one doubted if one was really hearing it at all: the note was so high-pitched that a subtler sense seemed called for.

There was only one window to the bakehouse, and that was by the door. For the rest, it was lit by a row of four 150-watt bulbs under plain conical shades.

All the dough was mixed by hand. There were two kneading-troughs of scoured wood in the centre of the room.

Blythely, a spare, balding man with a small pale moustache, was beating up a mixture in an earthenware bowl; his assistant, the blond-haired youth, was extracting flat tins of teacakes from one of the deep wall-ovens.

Both of their faces looked colourless and shone with sweat. A lock of the youngster's hair hung damp and limp over his forehead.

But most of all it was the heat that one noticed.

You walked into it as into a heavy liquid, surprised by it and temporarily thrown off-balance. For a moment your body stayed quiescent, unable to react. Then it prickled and began to perspire, after which the heat was real and could be accepted.

And the cricket, that was certainly a part of it.

The cricket's rattle sounded like the taunt of a heat-demon, the more mocking because you were unable to place it.

From everywhere and nowhere it chinked its jeering notes.

Blythely looked up but didn't cease beating his mixture. Perhaps he had seen Gently with Fuller and had guessed that he was a policeman. The assistant, now alternately sucking and shaking a burned finger, had obviously decided that the intruder was none of his business.

Gently moved deprecatingly down the bakehouse, unfastening his raincoat as he went.

'This is a hot shop you've got in here!'

Blythely sneaked another foxy little glance at him and kept on with his beating. His features were far from being attractive. He had a retroussé nose and a seamed, porous skin; his chin was small, his lips thin and colourless. He had given his age to Griffin as fifty-two, but he might easily have been ten years older.

'Is it always like this in here?'

'I should think so – in a bakehouse.'

'Doesn't it get you down sometimes?'

'I'm a baker, not a snowman.'

His voice was high-pitched with a note of querulousness. He spoke into his mixing-bowl, as though he were talking to himself.

'Anyway, you don't notice an east wind in here!'

Blythely said nothing.

'And with the summers we've been getting, I'd say you were better off than the next man . . . there'll be a lot of volunteer bakers if they keep on with the atom bombs!'

It was labour in vain as far as the baker was concerned. His face wore a fixed, neutral expression which was about as alterable as that of the Sphinx.

One imagined that it was a rare day when Blythely was caught actually smiling.

The assistant came over to enquire after some Madeiras in another oven. Quite unexpectedly the baker was now voluble, even jocose. He was showing off, probably, wanting Gently to notice his expertise – he treated the youngster to quite a sermon on Madeiras before he let him go.

'Some people don't realize what makes the difference.'

Gently contented himself with a sympathetic shrug.

'The average housewife today . . . well, there you are! It's no use telling them. They won't take the trouble. They shake some muck out of a packet with a pretty label, and wonder why their cakes aren't like mine . . .'

If beating was the secret, Blythely's cakes had nothing

to fear. With tireless regularity he kept slapping away at his creamy mixture.

'Are you the one they sent to London after?'

He was prepared to acknowledge Gently, having given the detective a taste of his quality.

'I saw in the paper that they'd run to the Yard. That's what I said would happen, right at the start.'

'There have been some developments which made it inevitable, Mr Blythely.'

'Which is to say it was London business, and nothing to do with us here.'

London business! The phrase conveyed a whole outlook. There was nothing important about London in Lynton. All that London did was to breed petty criminals, and when they upset Lynton you sent for a London copper.

Gently unbuttoned his jacket and passed a handkerchief over his brow.

The young assistant was pulling out the Madeiras, each with its garnish of peel; the aroma would have seduced an angel, but the heat destroyed any vestige of one's appetite.

Blythely had reached for a ladle and was beginning to dole out his mixture into paper-collared tins.

'Trying to find out what the others missed, are you?'

'That's roughly the idea . . .'

'We didn't notice anything here, I can soon tell you that.'

'All the same, you were here when the job was being done.'

'We were making up the buns. They could have delivered a whole cemetery. As far as I know, there was nothing stirring all night.'

Three ladlefuls went to a tin, and there was scarcely a speck remaining in the bowl. Blythely was still talking to the mixture as though Gently were a mere passing nuisance.

'I shall have to have more than that, I'm afraid.'

'Ted! Shove these Vanillas into number three, will you?'

'If you can spare me half an hour, Mr Blythely . . .'

Confound it, he was going on his knees to the fellow!

At last the baker condescended to notice his melting visitor. Hands on hips, he regarded him shrewdly with small hazel eyes.

'I've got to interrupt my work, have I?'

'Yes – if you *don't* mind.'

'You're wasting my time and yours, but I suppose that's the way they run things. We'd better go into the house before you turn into a grease-spot.'

The rub of it was that he was making Gently *feel* he was wasting the baker's time. Out here in the bakehouse real work was going on . . .

Blythely's sitting room over the shop struck a note of nostalgia. It had been furnished in the early thirties but the style was of ten years previous, this being the usual aesthetic gap between London and the provinces.

There were traces of *nouveau art* about the table and straight-back chairs. The three-piece suite was dumpy

51

and upholstered in leather, the arm-fronts being tacked with big brass-headed nails.

'Can I offer you something?'

Blythely had left his apron below stairs, seeming to have shed with it a great deal of his cross-grained authority. Up here he appeared awkward and more than ever colourless. The daylight gave a greyish tinge to the pitted skin of his face.

'No thank you . . . I'm on duty.'

'You won't mind me having a drop. At my trade you get a thirst – not that I ever touch alcohol, mind you.'

He went to the top of the stairs, which descended straight into the shop.

'Clara, bring me up a glass of that cold tea when you're at liberty . . .'

Through the muslin half-curtains Gently could watch the passers-by in Fenway Road. Well wrapped up, they still looked perished; the east wind was sweeping straight along the rather dingy thoroughfare.

'Take a seat, won't you?'

Gently turned one of the straight-backed chairs around so that he could straddle it.

'I realize you've got to do this – every man to his job. But the Good Lord knows that I had no hand in the business, nor, I feel certain, did anyone else in these parts . . .'

Gently made a wry face. 'That's what everyone says.'

'It's the truth, you'll find.'

'I hope you're right, Mr Blythely.'

The baker sat down stiffly, placing his hands on his

knees. Through the open door one could hear his wife chatting amiably to a customer in the shop.

'Go on – ask me your questions.'

Gently nodded without complying.

'You want to know when I started work – very well, it was a quarter to ten. Ted, he turned up at a minute or two after.'

'And you worked through till seven?'

'We had the bread to bake as well as the buns.'

'But surely you left the bakehouse once or twice?'

'The toilet is by the door.'

It was so simple and so convincing. There was nowhere to pick a hole in it. Fuller's story could be twisted and checked, but Blythely's was as unassailable as a block of concrete.

And you had to believe it, watching that plain, unemotional, unimaginative face.

Griffin had believed it, so why should not Gently?

'You're a chapel-goer, they tell me?'

'I am, and so is my wife.'

'You would not approve of horse racing, I feel sure.'

'It's an invention of the Devil.'

'Didn't you once keep a horse?'

Yes, he had had three. But the last one had been got rid of in 1938, since when the stable had been used as a junk repository.

'Mr Fuller uses the loft, he tells me.'

Was there just a flicker of reaction to that?

'I suppose he's never kept a horse there?'

Only too plainly, this was a wrong track.

Mrs Blythely appeared carrying the cold tea in a beaker. She was a handsome woman, and one wondered how she had come to throw in her lot with such an unpresentable husband.

She had deep golden hair only now beginning to fade, a slightly snubbed nose and lively green eyes. In her youth she must have been a ravishing beauty.

'Do I know this gentleman?'

Gently came in for a brilliant smile.

'I can guess who he is – only a policeman could get Henry out of the bakehouse! But he isn't the man who's been around such a lot.'

A good skin and an oval face, and a figure which was full but not yet going heavy.

The baker was lucky to have such a wife in his shop.

'Is the door on the latch?'

'Yes, my dear. And all the regulars have been.'

'This is the man from London. No doubt he's got something to ask you.'

With husbands and wives it was difficult to tell; they had an act to be put on for strangers, and the act was usually expert. Yet here, as with Fuller and his foreman, Gently had the impression of friction. He could scarcely have put his finger on any one spot, but the impression was none the less established.

'I went to bed soon after tea, Inspector. It's a long day in the shop – hard on the feet, too! As a rule I sleep like a log till my husband wakes me with a cup of tea. It was the same on Thursday night. I didn't remember anything after my head touched the pillow.'

Here again one had to believe it – difficult, even, to suggest the stock questions.

'No, I never get up during the night . . . the bathroom is next door, on the same floor.

'Naturally I go out by myself sometimes, but never away from Lynton. The only horse racing I've seen is on the newsreel . . . I entirely agree with what my husband says about it.

'I didn't see the – the man, but I'm quite certain that he was a stranger to me. The only Taylors we know are some people who keep a chemist's shop . . .'

Two worthy people who had been pursuing their lawful occupations. They had the truth to tell and they were comfortable in the knowledge of it.

'You sublet these premises from Mr Fuller, I believe?'

'That's right – and old Burge before him. I've been here twenty-seven years.'

'You're on good terms, I suppose?'

'What do you mean by that exactly?'

'Just a general enquiry.'

'We've never had a quarrel yet.'

Gently hesitated, catching it again, that subtle essence of something between the lines. Blythely was staring unwinkingly at the street, what was almost a frown had appeared on the face of his wife.

'By your standards, I suppose, Mr Fuller has rather lax principles?'

'Nobody has ever heard me criticize my landlord.'

'He drinks, doesn't he, and gambles sometimes?'

'I don't prescribe rules for him, and I'll let him know when he interferes with me.'

Oracular utterances, both of them, and pronounced with a degree of inflexible emphasis. Was it a warning to Mrs Blythely that this was the official line? She was compressing her lips as though keeping back an impatient comment.

'You're all local people, are you?'

'We are. Fuller comes from Starmouth.'

'Well, it's the same county!'

'Lynton's sixty miles from Starmouth.'

'And you've always got on well together?'

'He's a straight man of business.'

'But personally, I mean.'

'We aren't close friends, but we've never come to blows.'

Gently turned to Mrs Blythely.

'And you, you're on good terms, too?'

'But of course I am, Inspector!'

Yes, she was toeing the official line . . .

Gently suddenly felt tired of flogging a horse so patently dead. What did their little secrets matter, or even their skeletons, if they had any? Griffin was right, all along the line. He had cleared the way with commendable and faultless efficiency. Taylor was nothing to Lynton or Lynton to Taylor – one might as well face it, and stop annoying innocent people!

Wasn't the mill on the main through road, and open for every kid to wander around?

'*You* knew about the hopper of spoiled flour, didn't you?'

It was his parting shot, and he could hear its irritability.

'Ted told me about that. He heard some of the men talking. If Fuller had had his wits about him he would have spotted the diseased grain.'

'What about the foreman?'

'They were without one at the time.'

'Do you think Blacker is a good appointment?'

Blythely's face twisted into the only attempt at expression that Gently had witnessed.

'He is a Godless loafer, and conversant with the ways of the Devil.'

'Thank you, Mr Blythely, and forgive me for having detained you.'

He was not to get off so lightly, however. The fates seemed in a conspiracy to surfeit him with advocates of Lynton's innocency.

As he stood pondering in the mill yard a green Bentley drew up and out of it stepped a person with an air of considerable self-importance. He came straight across to Gently, his gloved hand outstretched.

'Chief Inspector Gently?'

'Yes, that's me.'

'My name is Geoffrey Pershore. I've just been talking to Superintendent Press. He told me that you were likely to be here, and I thought I should have a few words with you. I own this property, you understand, and can probably put you right about the characters of my tenants . . .'

Gently groaned in spirit, but was obliged to stand his

ground. Pershore was a bigwig in Lynton, and the super wouldn't thank Gently for hurting the gentleman's self-esteem.

'I expect you've come to the same conclusion as our men. This fellow was obviously murdered by his friends, who then hid the body in the mill. Fuller, I dare say, you are prepared to exonerate. Blythely I have known personally for twenty-five years . . .'

He was the true figure of a provincial 'great man', flanked by his Bentley and wearing expensive clothes which just missed being in taste. He would be in his middle fifties, perhaps, with a straight nose and a fleshy face flushed with good living. His blue eyes were watery and a little bloodshot. They had a habit of staring at you with sudden aggression, and then as suddenly swinging away again.

'Fuller is an excellent judge of character – I wouldn't seriously question a man he saw fit to employ. In addition to that, you must remember that I take an – ah – patriarchal interest in my investments. I would not allow anything to go on which had the merest breath of scandal attached to it. I have a reputation, Inspector . . . in confidence, I am expecting to be the mayor of Lynton next year.'

So that was the trouble, was it! Gently had to struggle to stop himself smiling. With the mayoralty in his grasp, Geoffrey Pershore had had the corpse of a racetrack crook planted in his moral mill . . .

'You can see the delicacy of my position, Inspector. I am not asking you to scamp your duty – I am a better citizen than that, I hope! But in making statements to the press . . . that sort of thing. If you could make it clear that the business was purely fortuitous, I would be *extremely* grateful.

'Any police charity in which you are interested, for example . . .'

It was little short of bribery. Gently really had to turn his head. In a moment, no doubt, he would be being promised letters of recommendation to his assistant commissioner and other such blameless favours . . .

'You can throw no light on the affair yourself, sir?'

It was a wicked thrust, and the popping eyes of the mayor-presumptive showed that he felt the sting.

'I . . . I – Good Lord, I wasn't even *in* Lynton at the time!'

'You have an alibi, have you?'

'A – a – yes, I suppose I have – if that's what you choose to call it! Thursday is my theatre night, and I was in Norchester. I arrived back at my house at about half past twelve – it is six miles out, on the Norchester Road. But honestly, Inspector—'

'I wouldn't want to scamp my duty.'

'I was never at any time suggesting—!'

'We like to clear up all the minor points, sir.'

Pershore goggled at him, his small mouth hanging half-open. He was obviously unused to being snubbed, even by the police; Gently felt almost sorry for the man's fish-like helplessness.

The situation was saved by the emergence of Fuller from the side door of his office.

'You're wanted on the phone . . . somebody called Dutt is asking for you.'

Gently hastened into the office and picked up the receiver. He seemed not to notice that Fuller and his landlord were closely attending him, and exchanging glances.

'Hullo, Dutt . . . what have you found?'

'Everythink, sir!' The cockney sergeant's voice had the childlike ring of excitement it took on when he had made a good killing.

'I found the place, sir – third flipping time of asking. It's The Roebuck – that posh place opposite the Abbey Gardens. Been there twelve days they had, spending money like water, then they checked out in a hurry on the Friday after lunch. And this is the cream of it, sir. Taylor's things are still in his room. They paid his bill in advance till the end of this week, which is the reason why nobody hasn't posted him as missing.'

Gently laid the receiver back softly on its rest. A faraway look had stolen into his eyes.

'You – you have had news, Inspector?' Pershore ventured, curiosity getting the better of affronted pride.

'Mmn.' Gently nodded. 'News I didn't expect . . . Lynton being the spotless town it is!'

'I beg your pardon, Inspector?'

Gently hunched his shoulders. 'Who knows? We may tie Lynton into it yet . . .'

When he was gone, he was certain, Pershore would ease his damaged feelings by taking it out on Fuller.

CHAPTER FIVE

THE ROEBUCK, LIKE the St George, had a large central courtyard in which stagecoaches had once changed horses, but in this instance it had been roofed with glass and now formed an extensive lounge. Tubs of palms flanked a central promenade carpeted in red and gold. From the roof depended wire baskets of ferns and geraniums. A cool, leisured, conservatory atmosphere penetrated the whole, and at this hour it had very few occupants.

Dutt was standing by the reception desk talking to the manager. Seeing Gently enter the sergeant clicked his heels and came across to meet his senior.

'What a bit of luck, eh, sir?'

'Good man, Dutt – you've beaten me to a lead!'

'Couldn't believe me ears, sir, when they says they recognized them. It just goes to show you mustn't overlook nothink . . .'

The manager came up, a worried-looking man with the appearance of an ex-army officer. He was very deferential and spoke in a low, conciliatory voice. From time to time he glanced at the one or two patrons who sat in the lounge conversing or reading the papers.

'I didn't much like these men, but what could I do? They had plenty of money, and there was nothing in their behaviour to which I could take a positive exception. They drank, of course, but so do a lot of guests, and you would soon lose your custom if you started being too precious about it.'

One got the picture at once. Another section of Lynton propriety had been injured by the impact of Taylor, Ames and Roscoe. They had been in funds and they had thrown their money about. They had drunk a lot of the best Scotch and at times had been noisy. Smutty tales had been told in the alien accent of Stepney . . .

'When they went I assure you I was relieved. I left orders that they were not to be readmitted, at least the two of them who had booked-out. It goes without saying that the names entered in the register bear no resemblance to those your sergeant mentioned.'

Biggs, Hawkshaw and Spenylove was the somewhat curious selection of aliases used. In each case the address given was that of a road in Finchley. Gently, who had rooms in that district, needed no convincing of the road's fictitious character.

'Did they have a car, these people?'

'They came and went in a taxi.'

'What about luggage?'

'According to the porter they arrived here with

nothing but a couple of Gladstones. They had suitcases when they left, expensive ones in solid leather.'

'What sort of money did they use?'

'I'm told they paid their bills in one-pound notes.'

'Did they drop any hint about where they were going?'

'They left no forwarding address. I have ascertained that the taxi took them to the station.'

'I'd like to see everyone who might have overheard some of their conversation.'

The manager's office at the side of the desk was impressed for this purpose. It was a small and accidental room with no windows and mechanical ventilation, the hissing whirr of the fan reminding one of below-deck cabins in ships.

The manager stood by unhappily as though to ensure that his staff gave the fullest satisfaction.

'This is Hayward who tends the bar . . . he will have seen a lot of them.'

'You remember these men, Hayward? Take a good look at the photographs.'

Slowly the picture began to take colour, the picture of three small-time rogues splashing about in a wonderful Pactolusean flood. Money they'd had, money to burn, money to throw away on food, drink, clothes, anything at all that took their fancy. They hadn't known what to do with it, so unused were they to such fabulous sums.

'They never tipped me less than a quid, and sometimes it was twice in an evening. "Don't bring me no

63

change," says one of them. "It spoils the set of my nice new trousies!"

'Another time they'd each of them bought a portable radio. They brought them into the bar and tuned them into three different stations at once.

'Then there were the electric razors – a lot of fun they got out of them. And one night they had a flashlight camera which must have cost them a hundred quid.'

Like children they had been, children who had been given the run of a toyshop. They had rushed to each new object with feverish delight, only to throw it away when something fresh caught their eye.

'The darkish bloke with the hard eyes bought a pair of binoculars made in Paris. The next day he'd got a better pair and he gave me the others.

'The little fellow couldn't get on with his razor and tossed with Harry, the night-porter, for it. He lost and handed it over. Bob, the waiter in the bar, came in for a wristwatch because it didn't happen to be a self-winder.'

Money . . . a bottomless well of it! And apparently they only been nibbling the outside edge. When Hayward had ventured a remark on it he was answered with broad winks. They were on to a good thing, they said, they had got their money on a winner-and-a-half this time . . .

'You never formed an impression of where that money came from?'

'I thought they'd got a system. They were always talking about horses. The dark bloke gave me one or

64

two tips, and all but one of them paid off all right. He knew his stuff when it came to the gee-gees.'

'They used to make bets, did they?'

'They never stopped making them. As often as not they'd be on the blower to someone at the course, and some flaming language got used when a nag let them down.'

'Did they mention a system?'

'No, not within my hearing.'

'What gave you the idea, then?'

'They used to have a conference over the papers every morning, and the dark bloke was working out something in his notebook. After that they got on the blower and placed their bets. Along with the lolly they chucked around, I reckoned it was a cert that they were working a system.'

There were no records of those calls; The Roebuck was equipped with pay-boxes for its patrons. Some mail had certainly arrived for one of the three men, but nobody could remember anything useful connected with it.

'Who did you see in their company?'

'Nobody that I can remember. They didn't try to be pally with the regulars.'

'How about women?'

The manager intervened.

'We don't permit that sort of person to be brought into The Roebuck . . .'

A porter was called, then a waiter and the chamber-maid. Stroke by stroke they added detail to the empty spaces.

'Were they ever away for the day?'

'They didn't miss a meal.'

'Would one of them have spent a night on the tiles?'

'They spent the evenings drinking and playing cards.'

'What about Thursday night?'

'It was just the same. The little bloke got up and went out at about half past eleven. The dark one said something to him and they all laughed like mad. The bar was closed, but they stopped there with a bottle of whisky between them.'

And he hadn't come back, the little bloke, he hadn't returned to pick up the jest and his glass again.

For a while the other two had taken no notice. They went on drinking and playing and smoking the Russian cigarettes which were temporarily in vogue with them. At one o'clock, however, they had sought out the night-porter.

'A bit anxious they seemed, wanted to know if their pal hadn't got back. No, I tells them, nobody hadn't come in since midnight. They went into a huddle, talking low so's I couldn't hear them, then the rough-looking one went up in the lift. When he came back they both of them went out. I reckon it was near on two before I saw them again.'

'Which way did they go when they left here?'

The porter sucked in his lips.

'Towards Fenway Road, I think it was.'

'And they returned from that direction?'

'I couldn't be sure. I'd got the kettle on, making myself a cup of tea.'

On returning they had put their question to him again. Now they were more than anxious, they were angry and apparently baffled. They remained another half-hour in the hall, conferring and casting black looks towards the door. Eventually they had given the porter a pound note and asked him to ring them if their friend turned up.

'Only that's what he didn't do, nor I haven't seen him since. The next day his mates booked out after lunch.'

In the morning they were having what sounded like a row in one of the bedrooms. The chambermaid had heard them at it and had caught a few phrases.

'They was calling somebody a little rat and saying that wringing his neck was too good for him. "What are you going to do about the stuff in the bank?" says one. "—something leave it there!" says the other. "What else can we do?"'

'That phrase . . . "wringing his neck" . . . you're sure about that?'

'Wring his neck or strangle him – it was one or the other.'

After breakfast they had been definitely off-colour. The routine of form-checking and bet-laying had gone quite by the board. The dark one had gone out, leaving his friend to bite his nails. When he returned, just at lunchtime, he had with him the noon edition of the evening paper.

'They never had their lunch at all. I saw them sitting in the bar with the paper on the table. They weren't talking, just sitting there – like as though something had knocked them all of a heap.'

And then, of course, they had gone, taking a taxi to the station; after paying their bill in one-pound notes, and ensuring that Taylor's disappearance wouldn't be prematurely reported.

Dutt had got hold of a timetable and was checking the afternoon trains. There'd been a London train at two fifteen, though the latest reports said they weren't back in Stepney.

'Do *you* do any racing?'

The manager looked startled.

'Well, as a matter of fact . . .'

'When was the last meeting at Newmarket?'

It chimed in exactly. It had been on the day when Taylor and his pals had arrived at The Roebuck. The booking had been phoned in, perhaps from the course; the elapsed time between booking and arrival coincided nicely with the times of the available train-service.

But what had occurred at Newmarket to send them hotfoot to Lynton . . . floating, almost, in an ocean of bank notes?

A mighty day at the races should have seen them carousing at Stepney! Unless, for some reason, Stepney had become suddenly unhealthy for them.

And since the police hadn't been looking for them, then it seemed to follow that . . .

'Ring up Newmarket, Dutt, and see what's been going on there. We're looking for a recent theft of bank notes, at or just before the last race meeting.'

The manager had lit a cigarette with hands which were trembling. One knew what he was going to say almost before he opened his mouth.

'I suppose there's bound to be publicity, Inspector?'

Wasn't that Lynton all over?

Gently grunted and turned his back on him – as though you could escape publicity in a business like this!

But there was nothing to be had from Newmarket, or nothing that looked like tying in. An empty house had been burgled a week before the races, a punter had been attacked and robbed as he left the racecourse.

'How much did they get off him?'

'Fifty quid, according to his statement.'

'We're looking for something bigger – probably several thousands.'

'Sorry, there's been nothing like that since a post-office van was held up four years ago.'

'Did you recover any of the money?'

'Yes, we got the lot.'

Yet they had had their money from somewhere . . . and that day at the races had been a crucial moment in the affair.

'Shall we take a look at his things, sir?'

Dutt, as always, wanted to be getting down to the practical.

'Yes, after which you'd better go to the station. There's just one chance in a hundred that somebody will remember where our two birds booked to.'

★   ★   ★

Taylor had enjoyed the luxury of one of the best rooms on the first floor. It was large and looked across the car park and street to the Abbey Gardens. Adjoining it was a small private bathroom with a shower, and a separate toilet.

That Taylor's belongings were still there was a factor made more important by the total absence of effects found on the corpse; while Griffin, for all his efficiency, had been unable to trace the reach-me-down clothes from which the makers' labels had been ripped.

'They've tidied the place up, sir.'

A lot of junk was lying about, but it had been put in order by the neat-handed chambermaid.

'I'll bet it was in a flipping mess when that geezer was living here . . .'

There was the portable radio, an expensive model with a chromium-plate interior; a table-lighter, a musical cigarette-box, a pair of Zeiss glasses hung carelessly from the bed-rail, a Leica that bore out the bartender's estimate. The wardrobe was stuffed with clothes of a type likely to appeal to the heart of the little Stepney spiv. On a bedside cabinet lay a pile of magazines featuring pin-up photographs. Two pigskin suitcases, still with labels attached to the handles, stood side by side in a corner.

'Went to town, sir, didn't he?'

Gently lifted the lid of the cigarette-box and absently picked out a cigarette. The Russian . . .

From the interior of the box tinkled an absurdly slow and fragile rendering of 'The Banana Boat Song'.

'Here, sir – look at this!'

Ferreting in the cabinet, Dutt had found a brand new bank book.

'Something new, isn't it, when these blokes bank their pickings?'

It was indeed. Gently took it with interest. It was issued by the local branch of the Westminster, three days after Taylor had arrived in Lynton; sixteen hundred pounds had been deposited, though progressive withdrawals had reduced the sum to twelve hundred and eighty.

A bank account too . . . could that money really have been come by honestly?

'This is a bit of a facer, Dutt!'

'Yes sir – isn't it?'

'He couldn't have been expecting any comeback if he put the stuff in a bank . . . it wasn't hot, and nobody was going to ask questions.'

'Like they really was working a system, sir.'

'Yes – only that leaves everything to be explained!'

In fact, the more one thought about it the less explicable it became. Unless the money were dishonest there had been no need for the trio to bury themselves in Lynton. The divisional police would have been interested and possibly irritating, but Taylor, Ames and Roscoe were no sensitive plants, and they would not have forsaken Stepney merely to avoid attentive policemen.

Yet who knew better than Taylor not to deposit dishonest money in a bank . . . ?

It was asking for trouble – almost guaranteeing it!

'Do you think he was going to bunk with it, sir, and the others rumbled him?'

Gently shook his head regretfully.

'It can't be that simple. If he were going to do a bunk he would hardly have left his bank book – and can you see the others letting him bank the stuff in his name? Besides' – he gestured to the scattered belongings – 'would he have just walked out on this?'

'He might have bought it all for a blind, sir.'

'You're overrating his intelligence.'

Taylor wouldn't have left his toys behind – toys he had spent a good proportion of that sixteen hundred on. 'There's a couple of points arising, though.'

Gently tapped the bank book.

'First there's the sum itself – what does that suggest to us?'

'Well, sir, it could be a share.'

'Exactly, Dutt. Which gives us the probable sum involved. It was five thousand pounds – Taylor banked sixteen hundred and kept the balance of sixty-six in his wallet. Then there's the date of the deposit.'

'You mean he didn't go to the bank the day after he got here, sir.'

'He didn't . . . which barely suggests that they didn't bring the money with them.'

'May I make a third point, sir?'

Gently shrugged. 'The floor's all yours!'

'Well, sir, from the way they was spending it – not to mention what they says to the bartender – it seems to

72

me that they was expecting some more. And that business wiv the list of bets sounds a cert for a system.'

'But it didn't pay off, Dutt – at least, there's only one deposit in Taylor's book.'

'Could've been an accumulator, sir, and they never seemed worried about it.'

Apart from swearing, of course, when a good thing failed to come up . . .

They went through the rest of Taylor's effects without fording anything to show for their pains. There were no documents except the bank book and some receipted bills; everything was new and without doubt purchased locally.

Down in the manager's office Gently recalled Hayward.

'This spending of money . . . was it the same all the time?'

'Yes, sir, just the same.'

'Even when they first arrived?'

Hayward thought for a moment.

'They may not have been quite so flush . . . the quid tips came later. But they were never close-fisted, I will say that for them.'

Which might mean that they didn't have the money or simply that they hadn't got into the way of spending it . . .

A strange business, altogether, and somehow rather a pathetic one. You caught the childish joy of these three rogues and their dream come true: money, safe if not honest, and almost respectability.

Wasn't that why Taylor had banked his share? Wasn't that perhaps his biggest luxury?

'Better take this to the bank and see what you can get from them.'

Gently handed the bank book to Dutt.

'Until we rope in Ames and Roscoe I can't see us making much headway . . . but we'll just have to keep on going through the motions.'

'Anyway, we've got somethink to show them, sir!' Dutt couldn't help feeling bucked by his success at The Roebuck. 'We've found out that they stopped here, which is more than the local boys did. And we know about the lolly, sir. We was only guessing before.'

Gently grunted and hunched his shoulders as they turned a corner into the grey east wind. He had a sensitive nostril for leads, and he couldn't smell one here.

What racket worth five thousand a squeeze could ever have taken root in Lynton?

CHAPTER SIX

'COFFEE OR TEA, sir?'
'Coffee!'

Gently almost growled at the middle-aged waitress, who in turn looked sullen. And to be truthful, there had been nothing to grumble at in either the food or the service.

He had had onion soup, which he liked, followed by a very good sole with sauce tartare. Then had come apple charlotte, which again he was fond of, and now he was eating Stilton cheese with biscuits. An excellent meal, served deftly and with promptness. Surely a smile should have rewarded the waitress?

Across the road another sort of lunch was being taken. Four of the mill workers were sitting on the pavement, their backs to the office wall, each with an open tin beside him. Their jaws worked slowly and they watched the passers with a naïve interest. Sometimes one of them would venture a remark, when the others would laugh raucously.

Earlier, Fuller had gone home in his neat Ford Consul. Then Mrs Blythely had slipped the latch of the shop door, trying it twice before she was satisfied it had caught. Next Blacker had come loping across, giving Gently a queer look, and finally Ted Jimpson, who had finished work for the day.

Ted had met a girlfriend, a sturdy little country wench. When a car passed Gently could see them reflected in the window-pane where they were sitting behind him. They, too, were glancing at him queerly, and apparently in a close conference together . . .

'Black or white, sir?'

'White – not too much milk.'

This time he made up for his surliness with a wink, and the waitress forgave him as far as to smile bleakly.

'Not a very nice day, sir.'

'At least it isn't raining.'

'Very dull, it's been, ever since Good Friday.'

Over the way a mill worker had seen him and was nudging his neighbour. Gently studiously avoided catching any of their eyes. He wanted them to see him, everyone connected with the mill. It never did any harm to let people feel you were still keeping an eye on them.

Nevertheless, he realized that it fell into the category of 'going through the motions' – he wasn't following a lead, or even, for that matter, a hunch.

A grudge, perhaps – that was another matter!

After getting a frozen reception at headquarters when he gave them the news about The Roebuck, he was feeling a perverse desire to hang Taylor's murder on Lynton's door.

They had been so smug, all of them, police and laity alike. And Press, though he hadn't actually torn him off a strip, had delicately rapped his knuckles for shouldering Pershore aside so roughly.

'You don't know what it's like, being in a small town like this one . . .'

He was wrong. Gently did. But it would have been pointless to have said so.

'In London Mr Pershore might not cut very much ice, but in Lynton I assure you . . .'

In Lynton you were a big-shot as soon as you started paying supertax.

Then there was Griffin, listening intently, and coming up with a cautious theory. 'Suppose he'd gone out to meet a woman, and her husband happened to find them?'

The trouble was that it was a tenable theory and one which ought to have crossed Gently's mind. The Blythelys were who Griffin was thinking about, and certainly the cap seemed to fit . . . if Taylor had been a Casanova, and setting aside the subsequent reactions of Ames and Roscoe.

Press, however, had sat down firmly on this scandalous interpretation of the facts. The mayor-elect had suffered enough without having further enormities fathered on him . . .

'Waitress, I'd like another cup of coffee!'

He had drunk the first one at a single gulp and was surprised to find the empty cup in front of him.

Blythely had come out into the mill yard and was standing staring at the pigeons. A van which momentarily hid the baker from view showed Ted Jimpson shaking his blond head and looking distinctly unhappy. What were they talking about, with their furtive glances at Gently's broad back?

Well, then, he had had a long talk over the phone with the assistant commissioner, the latter, no doubt, still twiddling his glasses and peering at the slice of Embankment across the courtyard. There hadn't been much comfort in that. The A.C. was still nursing his idea of a glorious, gilt-edged racket going on in Lynton.

'Have you thought of the docks, Gently? There's a lot of dope getting in these days . . .

'What about that chemical works outside the town? I see in the gazetteer that Lynton produces three per cent of the national supply of commercial sulphuric acid . . .'

It was too easy, sitting there in the Yard and turning over maps and reference books. One had to be in the place and get the feel of it . . . wasn't a betting system and Griffin's *crime passionel* the more likely idea of the two?

The assistant commissioner's information had been entirely of the negative variety. The division couldn't be quite certain when the three men had disappeared from Stepney, and Ames and Roscoe had not returned there. A round-up of likely elements had produced no worthwhile intelligence. There had been a notable silence in the world of narkdom.

'It's at your end, Gently, whatever it is. I feel sure that if you'll poke around a little more . . .'

'Would you like me to send you Simpson, of Anti-narcotics?'

He had asked for an all-stations and hung up feeling more depressed than ever. The arrival of an empty-handed Dutt had done no more than set the seal on his mood.

'There wasn't nothing at the station, sir – nobody didn't remember them. The bank manager sees Taylor, of course, and the cashiers remember him, but the lolly went to their headquarters and nobody did a check on it.'

'Pound notes was it?'

'Yessir. Sixteen bundles done up with rubber bands.'

'New notes or old?'

'They wouldn't swear to that, but one of them thinks they might have been new.'

'What about the other two?'

'They don't seem to have banked theirs, sir. I tried around the town, but there was nothink doing any-where.'

After which Gently had sat smoking in the office the super had allotted to him, indulging his blues and trying to pull something out of an empty bag . . .

There were two ends to the stick and he seemed to be holding the clean one. The dirty end, Ames and Roscoe, had disappeared like the eternal smoke-rings he was blowing. And the clean end was so very clean! There was scarcely a mark on it anywhere. Fuller's bare opportunity was the best it could show, coupled with the fact that the murderer seemed to have known his way about a mill . . . this mill, if the choice of hoppers was more than an accident.

Against that, where was the motive? What was Taylor to the Lynton miller?

They could have met at Newmarket. Taylor might have gypped Fuller . . . but would Fuller have then seen fit to strangle him, and to have hidden the body in one of his own flour-hoppers?

He could hardly have supposed that the business would pass as an accident!

Or put it the other way, to try everything: suppose Fuller had done the gypping. Suppose he had lost the astounding sum of five thousand pounds, and been pursued to Lynton and badgered for the payment . . . ?

Gently had shaken his head decisively – such a hypothesis was too fantastic! The miller would never have plunged to such a fabulous extent, or been able to produce such a sum on demand if he had. Moreover, having got it, Taylor and his associates would have departed to the happy haunts of Stepney.

Finally, there was the old chestnut of a racket. Once again you were dealing with a concept self-evidently academic. What could Fuller be running to produce pay-offs in the five thousand category – and how could Taylor and the others have cottoned on to it, meeting Fuller briefly on the racetrack?

Beside these extravagant theories Griffin's idea seemed a breath of sweet reason . . . it fitted most of the facts and did violence to scarcely any of them.

Who knew what charms the baker's wife had discovered in the little, rat-faced cockney?

Blythely had stopped staring at the pigeons and had come to the gate of the mill. Like the others, he had made out the bulky form of Gently sitting in the café window.

He said something to the workers, who had fallen silent at his approach; one of them laughed with a touch of self-consciousness, but the others remained serious enough.

'Still snooping around, is he?' – that would have been it. 'You want to watch out, together!' – and one of the workers had laughed.

Why were they constrained with Blythely – was it that they suspected something?

In the window he could see Ted Jimpson sitting bolt upright, his girlfriend watching him with lips which were compressed. Then somebody switched on the radio and the two of them relaxed their pose. A steel band was playing the calypso which Gently had heard tinkled out by Taylor's cigarette-box.

'A-working all night on a drink of rum,
Daylight's come and I want to go home . . .'

Gently drained his cup and signalled to the waitress, who was becoming resigned to his periodic refills. The café was emptying as the lunch hour wore on. Fuller, probably, would be back by two.

'You know the miller, do you?'

'Mr Fuller is often in here.'

'When was the last time?'

'He had lunch on Good Friday, the day they found the body.'

'Did he have a good appetite?'

The waitress obviously took this for a joke.

Now Blythely had turned his back and was going indoors with his jerky, obstinate stride. What would he have done, this man, faced with the situation Griffin had suggested? Was it in his awkward and self-righteous character to have become berserk and to have strangled the adulterer?

To have thrashed him, perhaps – 'chastisement' was the word that came to mind! – Taylor might certainly have had to expiate his sin through the flesh.

But strangling, that was another matter altogether. It suggested a fixed and calculated intent rather than a sudden outbreak of wrath. In addition to which he would have his wife to cope with. She might have reason to keep quiet – but dared he risk such a secret with her?

As always, one was brought up by a gross improbability. There weren't enough facts . . . that was the long and the short of it!

Gently helped himself to another lump of sugar and gulped down some more coffee. What was the residue of fact which didn't seem to link with the rest?

Well, there was Blacker and his relations with his master, and possibly the relations between the miller and Blythely. And then there was the stable, apparently a sore point with both the last two . . . though heaven alone knew how that could fit in.

Blacker, probably, was the most interesting to consider.

Hadn't he been made up to foreman on the day after the murder – a man antagonistic to his employer, and of doubtful competence?

That suggested pressure – and the timing was strangely coincidental. Blacker might have got a hint of something and put two and two together.

But if Fuller was the man, would he have straightway put the new foreman on emptying the hopper – giving himself, as it were, completely into the fellow's hands?

If it came to that, would Fuller have put it there at all? He could so easily have disposed of the corpse in some less damning spot.

So you were back where you started, floundering among the improbabilities. Wherever you picked it up the case handed you a *non sequitur*. It had been that way from the beginning, from the moment Taylor or one of his colleagues had lifted the phone and booked rooms in the stainless town of Lynton . . .

What could one do, except obstinately watch and wait?

'I beg your pardon, sir, but Ted . . .'

Gently looked up to find Jimpson's girlfriend standing uncertainly by his table. The blush on her rounded cheeks was becoming, and she had an appearance of wholesomeness, like an apple out of a cottage garden.

'What is it you want?'

'Ted here . . . we've been talking it over . . .'

Ted Jimpson had wandered into the background, a hangdog expression on his palish face.

'Well, sir, we thought he ought to tell you . . .'

'Go on, then . . . I won't bite!'

'. . . he wasn't there that night – not *all* the time, that is! He come out to see me home. I was working late shift in the caff.'

Gently sat them down at his table, Jimpson in front of him and the girl to his right. The workers across the way, who had been about to retire into the mill, hesitated to witness this new disposition.

'Let's get it straight . . . we're talking about the Thursday evening, are we?'

Jimpson nodded, swallowing at the same time.

'When according to Mr Blythely you showed up at ten – and remained in the bakehouse until seven the next morning?'

'Yes, sir, but . . .'

'But Mr Blythely is a liar?'

'No, sir – I didn't say so!'

'Then what am I supposed to believe?'

'He – he wasn't in there at the time.'

Gently folded his arms on the table and appeared to consider the hotel-plate sugar bowl. Was this the something he had been looking for, the little crack in the solid Lynton defence?

Jimpson was writhing in his chair, haplessly aware of the significance of what he had blurted out. In the background the radio continued its programme of calypsos.

'Go on – tell me what happened. I suppose it's no use asking why you didn't tell this to Inspector Griffin?'

'I didn't want him to know . . . Mr Blythley, I mean! And he didn't say nothing about having been out . . .'

'Did he tell you not to mention that?'

'No, but I thought . . .'

'Never mind about that, just get on with your story.'

It was simple enough and easily corroborated. Jimpson had met his girl, Jessie Mason, when she had finished her shift at the Globe Café at half past eleven. Her way home took her past the mill. He had slipped out and intercepted her. At her house, ten minutes away, he had exchanged greetings with her father, and had been back in the bakehouse at just on midnight. And during all that time Blythely had been absent, neither did he return until half an hour later.

'You're sure of those times?'

'Yes, I was looking for a chance . . .'

'He went out shortly before half past eleven?'

Jimpson nodded his head.

'Where did he say he was going?'

'He didn't say nothing.'

But he had gone out into the yard, Jimpson thought, because there had been no squeak from the broken hinge on the door to the shop. After waiting a few minutes he had ventured into the yard, and not seeing Blythely, had hurried out to meet Jessie.

'Was he in the habit of going out like that?'

'No, he wouldn't never leave the bakehouse as a rule. Once you've got the dough rising . . .'

'What did he say when he came back?'

'Nothing, he didn't.' Jimpson looked sideways.

'Go on, Ted!' urged Jessie. 'You said you was going to tell him everything.'

'Well . . .' Jimpson hesitated. 'He was something upset, that's all I can say. First off he was quiet, then afterwards he let me have it. I didn't know whether I was coming or going.'

'Had he seen you go out?'

'Not him, or I'd have heard about it.'

'What was he angry about?'

'Every mortal thing I did.'

Gently slowly nodded, still watching his sugar bowl. This had to be true in substance . . . unless there was a conspiracy against Blythely! But there might be an explanation, sufficient if not innocent: Blythely might have had the misfortune to go out on business he wanted to keep quiet.

'You corroborate this?'

Jessie's pretty flush came back. 'Of course I do – it's every word the truth!'

'What's your father's job?'

'He's a gardener with the Corporation.'

'Up late last Thursday, wasn't he?'

'He *always* waits up when I'm on the late shift.'

'Where did he become acquainted with Mr Blythely?'

'He hasn't never met him that I ever heard of.'

'A betting man, is he?'

'No fear! He's very strict about everything like that.'

He would be, naturally, if he was employed by the Lynton Corporation . . .

Out of the corner of his eye Gently saw Fuller's Consul draw up, hesitate, and then turn carefully into the mill-yard gate. The miller climbed out, reaching after him a leather briefcase. As he closed the door his eye fell on the café window: for a moment he stood quite still, an expression of blankness on his bold-featured face.

'Just before Mr Blythely went out . . . what happened then?'

'We were getting up the dough . . .'

'Did you hear the hinge squeak, for instance?'

'I wasn't listening for it.'

'What was Mr Blythely doing?'

'He was kneading the . . .'

'Which trough was he using?'

'The one near the door.'

Fuller came suddenly out of his trance and flung angrily into his office. Even in the café one could hear the slam of the door. His face appeared a few seconds later, peering over the screen, along with it that of his not-unattractive clerk.

'Who else was around that night?'

'Who . . . ? Nobody!'

'Who was in the yard when you got back?'

'I tell you—!'

'You didn't go straight into the bakehouse, did you?'

'Yes, I did!'

'What's the quarrel between Mr Blythely and Mr Fuller?'

'There isn't no quarrel – they get on all right together!'

Gently shrugged and drank off the rest of his coffee. He was giving poor Jimpson a rough sort of a passage, but then he shouldn't have been such a silly young . . .

'What else haven't you told the police?'

'Nothing, I tell you!'

'Why did you come to me just now?'

'Jessie and me . . . she thought I ought to!'

'What have you got against Mr Blythely?'

'Nothing I haven't! He's all right to me . . .'

'You'd better think carefully if there's anything else you want to tell me.'

The café now was practically empty; Gently's waitress stood at a distance by a sideboard, pretending not to be interested. A sunny West Indian voice from the radio was unfortunately spoiling her chances of eavesdropping.

'Cricket, lovely cricket . . .
At Lord's where I saw it!'

Only one customer was left, but he, as it happened, was sitting at the table immediately behind Gently.

'You can add nothing, Miss Mason?'

'Only that Ted's telling you the God's truth.'

'You must have passed the junction of Cosford Street

88

with Fenway Road – did you notice anyone making use of the back passage to the drying-ground?'

'No, I didn't.'

'Or anyone about there?'

'No.'

'A parked car, perhaps?'

She shook her head and then stopped herself. 'There was a car there, come to think of it. I noticed one standing off the road just down Cosford Street.'

'What sort of car, Miss Mason?'

'I don't know – I just saw it. It hadn't got no lights on.'

'A saloon car, was it?'

'I suppose so. I just saw it standing there.'

Gently sighed to himself. If only women paid more attention to cars . . . ! But there it was, another tiny fact, to fit, it might be, a final pattern.

'Righto . . . that's all for just now, though I shall probably need a statement from both of you later.'

A bit shakily they rose from the table – it had been a good deal worse than either of them had expected! Jessie stuck her hand defiantly into Ted's, and wordlessly they passed out through the doorway.

Young love . . .

Wouldn't she make him a very good wife?

'Waitress – I think I'll have some tea this time!'

Gently turned about and tapped the shoulder of the customer behind him.

'Don't be shy, Mr Blacker . . . come and sit at my table. I feel we could profitably discuss the situation.'

CHAPTER SEVEN

WHY HAD GENTLY'S mood changed, out of all proportion to the progress he was making? He couldn't have given the answer himself, certainly not in the cold terms of an official report.

Nothing else had changed in the small café or the street outside. Over in his office Fuller was still peering across his screen, further along Mrs Blythely had lifted the latch of the shop door and now leant, elbows asprawl, scanning a lunchtime paper at her counter. From the loudspeaker above the serving-hatch the calypso singer continued to celebrate the deeds of 'those little pals of mine':

'Cricket she makes so much fun . . .
The second Test and the West In'ies won!'

Yet his mood had changed radically. He had a tingling feeling of suppressed excitement. Something, surely, was on the move . . . he was beginning to get hold of the end of the stick in his hand!

'Never mind your cup – the waitress won't mind seeing to it.'

Blacker had somehow overturned the cup containing the dregs of his coffee, and was now trying to mop them up with a paper serviette.

'You might have given us a warning . . .'

'I didn't know you were sensitive.'

'Anyway, I got to get back.'

'I feel certain that Mr Fuller can spare you for a bit.'

The foreman, recovered from his violent start, didn't seem unduly discomposed. He lounged untidily into the chair beside Gently and lit a cigarette taken from an old tobacco tin.

'So what do you want to know, then?'

If anything, his tone sounded complacent.

'Whatever you can tell me.'

'P'raps you think I could tell you a lot, eh?'

'Perhaps.'

Blacker puffed deliberately at the cigarette, holding it between his finger and thumb with an air of clumsy affectation. Then he gestured with it towards the window.

'See who's watching us over there?'

Gently nodded.

'Don't think he likes seeing us two together – what are you going to make out of that?'

The green-grey eyes met Gently's cunningly and a smirk twisted the weak mouth. There was nothing prepossessing about Blacker – even his ears seemed stuck on as an afterthought.

'How long have you worked at the mill?'

'Six years I reckon – six years too long.'

'There must have been others who've worked there longer.'

'Ah, but then I've got influence, you see!'

Gently nodded again, but made no further comment. If Blacker wanted to be clever, he was prepared to give him scope. Meanwhile there was Fuller, frozen behind his screen; at the distance one couldn't read the expression, but one could see the unnatural pallor . . .

'The boss and me, we're like two brothers – in each other's pockets, as you might say. When it happened he wanted a foreman, why, there I was. "Sam," he said, "you'd better take over." Just you ask him if that wasn't the way of it.'

'And that was on Good Friday?'

'W'yes, why shouldn't it be?'

'I understood that Mr Fuller was without a foreman before that date.'

'Ah, but he couldn't carry on like that – it was too much for him, he had to give in.'

Blacker was quite happy now, puffing away at his cigarette. His whole clumsy attitude was one of complacency – of patronage, almost. He was conferring favours on Gently.

As he smoked he tilted back his chair with his heels. His big-boned frame, all knobs, showed up through the dusty drill trousers and jacket he was wearing.

'The boss, now, he's one of the best . . . when you get to know him! Some people says he's got a temper, but don't you believe it. Nervous he is sometimes – aren't we all now and then? – but underneath it there's a heart of gold. I reckon they don't come better than Harry Fuller, there . . .'

'What about Mr Blythely?'

'Huh?'

Blacker was unprepared for the change of subject.

'I was asking what was your opinion of Mr Blythely.'

'Oh, *him*! Well, that's another kettle of fish entirely.'

The smirk came back to the foreman's lips, but this time it wasn't directed at Gently. A private joke it seemed to be, a secret amusement of Blacker's maliciousness . . .

'Now *he*'s a queer bird if you like, with his hymn-singing and Bible-thumping. Don't drink, don't swear – you'd hardly believe he did the other thing! Wouldn't surprise me if he couldn't, neither, judging by results. Been married twenty years, they have . . . do you reckon the bakehouse has anything to do with it?'

Gently merely shrugged and stared absently through the window. Unaware of being observed, the buxom Mrs Blythely was wrapping loaves in tissue for a customer.

'Well, he's a bloke I'd keep an eye on if I was a policeman. You never can tell where these holy-boys are going to finish up. They keep it all bottled in – don't tell me that's natural! – then one of these days . . . Yes, I'd keep an eye on him!'

'Why did he quarrel with Mr Fuller?'

'Huh?'

Blacker was brought up short again, letting his chair come halfway forward.

'Didn't know they had quarrelled – not yet, anyhow. Daresay they will do, though, before they've finished with each other.'

'What do you mean by that?'

Blacker looked suddenly wary.

'Why, it stands to reason . . . old Blythely's got a nasty tongue. One day he'll say something that Harry won't take from him. Harry ain't no saint, you know, he don't go round preaching sermons.'

'Likes his pint and his fun, does he?'

'Yes – one of the lads, he is.'

'Might raise a bit of scandal.'

'Well, there you are . . . that woman who does the letters for him. Though, mind you, she's a toffee-nosed bitch. Wouldn't look at the likes of me and the rest of them. But you can take my word' – Blacker winked knowingly – 'she wouldn't say no if the right person asked her. You can always tell about bits of stuff, eh?'

He rocked the chair, watching Gently closely. The man from the Central Office appeared to be studying infinite distances. Blacker ran his tongue over tobacco-stained lips.

'Not that I want to say a word against Harry – see? He's a good pal to me, you can say what you like about him. So I know how to hold my tongue. If I sees anything I just keep my eyes shut. And Harry, he appreciates it – he knows that he can trust me! Which is why he made me his foreman when he found he couldn't get on without one.'

'Is he trusting you now, sitting here talking to me?'

Blacker tried to smirk, but a wryness had got into it. He darted a glance through the window at the spectral face of his employer.

'I didn't mean nothing by that, just pulling your leg! Blast, this business is enough to make anybody get edgy.'

'Where does the stable come into it?'

'The stable . . . ?'

Blacker's chair fell forward.

'The stable at the back there . . . don't tell me you don't know about it!'

This time he had got home with a vengeance. There was no complacency in Blacker's manner now. He stared stupidly at Gently, his long face longer still; for two whole seconds he could only open his mouth and gape helplessly.

Mrs Blythely, from her shop door, looked a moment in their direction. But then she seemed to shrug and went back to poring over her newspaper.

'What about it . . . that there stable?'

'That's what I'm asking you.'

'Don't know what you mean . . . the stable! What's it got to do with me?'

'Not only with you, but also with Messrs Fuller and Blythely.'

'It's their stable, isn't it? What am I supposed to know about it?'

They were calling each other's bluff, and both of them were aware of the fact. Gently had touched a chord which threw Blacker on the defensive, but he was giving nothing away until he could see what cards were being held . . .

'Harry keeps some hay up there – that's all *I* can tell you! If you want to know anything else, then I reckon you'd better ask him.'

'I've asked him already and now I'm asking you.'

'Well, I don't know nothing, and that's the fact of the matter.'

Gently brooded a second over his empty teacup, then he produced a ten-shilling note and tossed it down on the table.

'Come on!' he said. 'Let's go and look it over. The sight of the place may improve your memory . . .'

Protesting, Blacker allowed himself to be led out of the café. At least a dozen pairs of eyes were on them – even Blythely was watching from a window high up above the bakehouse.

Just as they went past it the side door of the office opened, but Gently was looking neither to the right hand or the left.

'In you go – it isn't locked. We'll take a look at this side first.'

The stable was a double one with the loft over the inward compartment. Lit by no windows it was gloomy enough, but Blacker pushed in as though he knew his way about. He came to a sullen standstill amongst a raffle of packing-cases and broken chairs.

'What happens now?'

'Pull that rubbish to one side.'

'There's nothing behind that . . .'

'Never mind – pull it aside!'

Blacker was right, there was nothing behind it, with the exception of spiders and a great deal of litter. The floor beneath was of corrugated black tiles, sunk a little at the centre for the purpose of drainage.

'Satisfied now?'

'Shift the rubbish on the other side.'

'I tell you it's a waste of time . . . !'

But the rubbish was duly removed, yielding the same result as before.

'How do you get into the loft?'

Blacker indicated a wooden fodder-trough at the end of the compartment. A packing-case stood by it by way of a step, and above, in a wooden dividing wall, two planks had been left out to provide a means of ingress.

'Right – up you go!'

Blacker swung himself up with ungainly grace. The loft smelt fragrant with the scent of clover hay, several bales of which lay stacked by the loading door. In addition to this there was a pile of barley straw; it was making a lot of itself and covering much of the floor-space.

'Move those bales, will you? I'll turn over the straw.'

There was a pitchfork standing by the wall, and Gently showed that he knew how to use it. Blacker, resigned to the futility of protest, quickly tumbled apart the heap of wire-bound hay bales.

Nothing, and again nothing.

The smirk was creeping back to the foreman's lips.

'What did you expect to find – somebody else strangled? I reckon there was only that one . . .'

'What's this – a new sort of horse-brass?'

Gently bent down and picked out something from the tousled straw. It was a tiny gold cross, measuring not more than an inch in length. He held it up so that Blacker could see it.

'Something you know about or something you don't?'

'What, me! What should I know about it? I aren't never up here.'

'All right . . . don't labour it!' Gently shrugged and dropped the cross into his pocket. 'We'll get on to our next port of call – perhaps it will be a little more productive.'

Blacker scowled at him suspiciously. 'I'm not going nowhere else.'

'Oh yes.' Gently nodded. 'You've begun to rouse my interest. I think we ought to check on that woman of yours . . . don't you?'

Coming out of the stable they had run into Fuller. The miller had followed them along the passage and now stood, a picture of desperate indecision, some yards from the stable door. Blacker tried to catch his eye and failed absolutely. Gently, who might have had better luck, appeared to be unaware of Fuller's existence . . .

The unhappy man followed them with his eyes until they turned out of the upper passage into Cosford Street.

'There's a lot of work on this afternoon . . .'

Blacker's anxiety was increasing by leaps and bounds.

'I don't care if you see Maisie – I haven't got nothing to hide! But why can't I just tell you where to find her, and you let me get on with my job . . . ?'

Gently, however, seemed to have added deafness to his visual affliction.

Lynton was dead on that chilly afternoon. The east wind had swept the streets as cleanly as a corporation road-sweeper. Looking in the shops, you saw the assistants talking together or leaning bored at their counters; you marvelled that it was worth anyone's while to pretend to have a business there.

In the square the stallholders looked perished and miserable, and even the pigeons had retired to fluff their feathers somewhere else.

An east wind in Lynton . . . what lower depths could one plumb?

'What time did you visit this woman?'

Gently broke a long silence as they drew opposite the police station.

'I met her in The Fighting Cock – you know what I told them! We went round to her place when the pub closed at half ten.'

'What had you done before that?'

'Before that . . . ? What I always do! I went home and got my tea, then had a wash and got into my pub-crawling outfit.'

'Is she a regular of yours?'

'Off and on, as you might say.'

'How long have you known her?'

'I don't know – ten years, p'raps.'

'Local, is she?'

'You wouldn't think so when she opens her mouth.'

'Has she been in trouble with the police?'

'No, she haven't, or she'd have told me.'

'Has Mr Fuller ever met her?'

'How should I know who he's met?'

Out of the square they took a street leading into the dock area. It was an ugly district of narrow thoroughfares and rows of houses built of dirty yellow brick. Aspidistras flourished in the windows, filling the gap between draped lace curtains. Now and again, as they passed, a curtain would be twitched by an anonymous hand.

'How long have you been interested in horses?'

'I don't know – who said I was interested?'

'You bet on them, don't you?'

'You can't pinch me for that!'

'Did this woman go with you to Newmarket that day?'

'I never went to Newmarket – haven't been there in my life.'

'With whom do you lay your bets?'

'Nobody ever said I laid any.'

To the left lay the warehouses with the quays behind them – small, unextensive, but adequate to handle the few small tramps touching in with timber and coal.

The sea didn't touch Lynton; it was served by a muddy estuary. One picked up a pilot a long way out to bring a ship through the labyrinth of shoals.

'What time did you leave her on Friday?'

'Maisie? Time enough to get to my work.'

'Who else is she friendly with?'

'You'd better ask her.'

'Sailors, perhaps?'

'All the girls pick them up.'

'You should know if she's got a regular.'

'Well, I don't, and that's the fact.'

Blacker was jumpy now and he couldn't hide it. He kept trying to read the expression on Gently's stolid countenance.

'What other pubs do you go in?'

'All of them – I aren't particular.'

'When were you last in The Roebuck?'

'The last time I was a millionaire!'

'How about your girlfriend – does she ever go there?'

'It's likely, isn't it – living in a dump like this!'

They had turned into a gloomy cul-de-sac guarded by a solitary lamp post, a nameplate on which bore the designation: Hotblack Buildings. A brick wall closed in one side and a ramshackle store the end. The row of houses, each projecting a solitary worn step to the pavement, had a blind, eyeless appearance, as though they had ceased trying to look the world in the face.

Halfway along a begrimed infant was sitting in the road, frowning as it tugged at the spring of a broken toy; it seemed unaware of its frozen fingers and smiled at the two men.

'Which is her house?'

'The one at the end.'

Gently had to knock twice before he got a reply.

The door, opened cautiously, revealed a woman of uncertain age, a dressing-gown thrown hurriedly about her plumpish shoulders.

'Chief Inspector Gently of the Criminal Investigation Department . . . I'd like to have a few words with you, ma'am.'

She stared over his shoulder at the lagging Blacker.

'About him again, is it? I've been through all that before!'

Inside the house was even more depressing than without. The street door opened straight into a small, icy room, its single window providing a totally inadequate light.

On the floor was worn linoleum patterned to look like parquet. The three-piece suite, upholstered in brown rexine, appeared too small for the actual practice of sitting.

'Don't you coppers trust one another? The last one wanted to know the inside of a maggot's behind! And as for Sam being mixed up in that business at the mill—!'

A little too shrill, was it . . . a little too aggressive?

Gently seated himself massively, his hips nipped between the narrow arms of the chair. Not for the first time he wondered what men saw in this sort of woman . . .

'Your name is Maisie Bushell, is it?'

'Of course it is – do I look like Marilyn Monroe?'

She looked more like a Blackpool landlady, with her domineering chin and pugnacious green eyes.

'Are you a Lynton woman, Miss Bushell?'

'Yes, I am, if you must know.'

'You've lived all your life in Lynton?'

'Course I have – didn't the others tell you?'

'You've never stayed in London, for instance?'

'Stayed there! I've never even seen the stinking place! What are you getting at, mister – what am I supposed to have done now?'

'Won't you sit down, Miss Bushell? This may take a little time.'

She dumped herself on to the settee, never once taking her eyes off him or glancing at Blacker. The foreman, after hanging about by the door for a little while, folded his bony frame into the other chair and put on an expression of exaggerated unconcern.

'Now . . . about what happened on last Thursday evening. Would you mind going through it again for my benefit, Miss Bushell?'

'There isn't nothing to go through. Sam spent the night with me. We've been pals a long time, you don't want to think that every Tom, Dick and Harry . . .'

'How long have you been friends?'

'How should I know? Years—!'

'And he is in the habit of spending the night here?'

'Why shouldn't he, if he wants to?'

'Last Thursday . . . was that by arrangement?'

'No, it wasn't. I just ran into him.'

'Start from there, if you please, Miss Bushell. Just tell me everything that happened.'

Now she did throw a quick look at Blacker, but the

foreman was gazing fixedly at the empty bars of the fireplace.

'Well, I went down town like I always do – I'm not one for staying in of an evening! And I had a drink at The Craven Arms, and another one at The King's Head. Then I went on to The Three Cocks, where I saw Sam here sitting on his lonesome—'

'Just a moment, Miss Bushell . . . what street is that in?'

'It isn't in any street. It's in Junction Road.'

'And The Fighting Cock – where's that?'

'What's that got to do with it?'

'According to Mr Blacker it was there that he met you.'

She stared at him angrily as though he were trying to pull a fast one. Then she jerked her head commandingly in Blacker's direction.

'Why can't you remember instead of telling the man a fib! You know it was The Three Cocks – I've told them that all along!'

'It just slipped out, Maisie . . .'

Blacker stirred his feet embarrassedly.

'And now you've got him thinking I'm telling him a lot of lies!'

'Whoa!' interrupted Gently. 'Let's have the correct version, shall we? Is The Three Cocks simply what you've been telling the police, or is it in fact where the meeting took place?'

'It's where I met Sammy.'

'You're sure about that?'

'Course I'm sure about it! What does it matter, anyhow? We went to several places – could have been The Fighting Cock amongst the rest of them.'

'But Mr Blacker says you stopped in one public house!'

'And I say we didn't! Him . . . he's got a memory like a sieve – mixing it up with another night, that's what *he's* been doing!'

'That's right!' chimed in Blacker. 'Now it's just dawned on me. It was Saturday we was in The Fighting Cock, Maisie. But I got it right when the bloke was taking it down . . .'

Gently sighed and felt for his pipe. It was symptomatic, perhaps, but they'd soon get the story squared up again.

'What public houses did you visit?'

'As if I'd remember! But I dare say we finished up in The Dun Cow, being on the way here.'

'They'd remember you there?'

'Don't see why they shouldn't.'

'What time did you get home?'

'After they turned out – we come straight back.'

'And neither of you went out again?'

'Sam didn't leave here till the eight o'clock news was on.'

'And you, Miss Bushell?'

'Don't ask a stupid question!'

'I'd appreciate a straight answer . . .'

'All right – I stinking well didn't!'

She was undoubtedly the stronger character of the

two, sitting bolt upright in her dressing-gown on her comfortless settee. Blacker had automatically accepted a secondary role. His memory wasn't so good . . . and that was dangerous, in a liar!

Gently filled his pipe with slow care and lit it with a couple of matches. The narrow chair made him feel as though he were in a straitjacket, and the chill of the room was sending shivers up his back.

'Have you ever been to Newmarket, Miss Bushell?'

'Dare say I have at one time or another.'

'Recently, have you?'

'No, I haven't – and what's that got to do with it?'

'Do you know any of these men?'

He flashed his set of photographs.

She lingered over them boldly, but if she recognized any of them she gave no indication of it.

'You know The Roebuck, of course?'

'Why shouldn't I know it?'

'Have you been in there during the last fortnight?'

'Don't make me laugh, copper!'

'The mill too . . . you'll know that? Have you been round the back – into that stable, perhaps?'

Once more it scored a hit, that apparently harmless building. You could almost hear Blacker holding his breath in the silence following the question.

'What stable . . . what do you mean? I don't know nothing about stables!'

'Not the stable behind the mill, Miss Bushell?'

'No, I don't – I haven't never been there!'

'Then this wouldn't belong to you, would it?'

Gently suddenly produced the little gold cross.

'You wouldn't have dropped it there on Thursday night – when you were entertaining somebody in the hayloft?'

The moment of silence had a different quality this time. Instinctively Gently could feel that he had played his card wrongly. They were still scared, both of them, he was on or around the target, but the tension had subtly relaxed a few degrees.

'Don't know what you're talking about, copper!'

'Maisie was with me – you ask them round the pubs.'

'I never went near the mill, and you can't prove I did. As for that cross thing—!'

'She never had one of those.'

Gently smoked expressionlessly through the clamour of denial. He was wrong, and they were relieved, and the relief betrayed itself in the fervour of their disclaimers.

But he hadn't been far wrong – that was the point! There was a guilty link between this pair and the stable, and through that with Blythely and Fuller.

Could the stable have been the scene, and Blacker, say . . . hadn't Fuller made him foreman?

'Look here – this is an offer.'

He blew a stream of smoke across the dingy room.

'If you've been concealing knowledge of this business it's a pretty serious affair. You're both liable to be indicted as accessories after the fact – which means a stiff sentence if you happen to be convicted.'

'But if you come clean now I'll do what I can for you.

It may be that you'll get off with nothing more than a warning. So suppose you do the sensible thing, and tell me what you're hiding?'

'But we ain't hiding nothing!'

Maisie's battleship chin lifted.

'How many more times do we have to . . . I tell you, we don't know a bloody thing!'

'And you?' Gently turned to Blacker.

'I've told you everything *I* know!'

'I'm making you both a good offer . . .'

'Now isn't that sweet of a stinking cop!'

'Right, then!' Gently levered his tortured hips out of the chair. 'We'll do it the hard way, since that's how you want it – from now on you can consider yourselves as being under surveillance. You won't leave Lynton and you'll hold yourselves available for questioning. And heaven help you if we find that you know a fraction more than you've told us!'

He didn't slam the door, which seemed unlikely to survive such a gesture; but the panache of his exit suggested that a door had been slammed.

CHAPTER EIGHT

'Paypor – paypor! latest on the Mill Murder!'

Gently bought a copy from the vendor shivering by the market stalls.

'victim guest at local hotel – Police favour "double cross" theory – "All-Stations" alert for associates.

'Latest developments in the investigation of the murder at Lynton of Stephen ("Steinie") Taylor have led the police to one of the town's most celebrated old Coaching Inns . . .

'In an interview this morning with Chief Inspector Gently of the Yard, who is conducting the investigation, our reporter was told that the facts justified the theory that Taylor . . .'

And there was the picture of Gently outside the hotel, making him look like a congenital idiot.

Soon the grey streets would be lively with the factory workers, grabbing their papers as they hurried in to tea. Did they believe them, these glossied accounts, with their factual-sounding guesses? Over kippers in the kitchen, would they pass current for the truth?

He tucked the paper into his pocket and plodded across the square to headquarters. As he pushed through the swing doors the sergeant on the desk nodded to him respectfully.

'Has my man left a message?'

Gently had sent Dutt to poke around the docks.

'Yes, sir, soon after lunch. He rang up from the railway station, sir.'

Nothing if not thorough, Dutt had returned to the station to question some of the staff he had missed earlier. As a result he had found a booking clerk who remembered the departure of Ames and Roscoe.

'He said to tell you they booked singles to Ely, sir. They were first-class tickets, and the two chummies seemed to be in a big hurry. They went off on the two fifteen London.'

'Ely, was it?'

Gently made a face. From Ely one could take a train to almost anywhere else in the country.

'Doesn't give you much scope, sir.'

The sergeant sounded sympathetic.

'No – but you'd better get on to Ely for me and see what they can dig up. Oh, and if my man comes in . . .'

'Yes, sir?'

'. . . tell him I've got a tail job for him, and fix him up with a bike. I want him to keep tabs on the foreman at the mill – obvious tabs. I want the fellow worried.'

The mood was still with him, the mood of confident

expectation. He'd got his teeth into something, whatever that something was.

On his way back to the mill he turned aside into the drying-ground, pausing again before the enigmatic stable.

There was nobody to be seen there now. The place had a sleepy, neglected atmosphere; all the buildings around seemed to have turned their backs on it. The thumping of the naphtha engine, subdued and asthmatical, owned something of the quality of the cricket in Blythely's bakehouse.

Wasn't it the perfect spot for an assignation . . . or a crime? It was overlooked by nothing except the bleary windows of the mill's posterior.

He passed on down the passage. In the engine-room two men were standing, apparently engaged in earnest conversation. One of them, the silent one, was the miller; the other – Gently sighed – was Lynton's egregious mayor-elect.

If only the fellow would leave his tenants to stew in their iniquity!

'Ah . . . Inspector!'

Pershore had caught sight of him and came strutting out of the engine-room.

'I've been on the phone – the superintendent informed me of your magnificent progress. Allow me to congratulate you, my dear fellow. I was sure that Press would get a good man down!'

Gently mumbled something, but his eyes were fixed on Fuller. If ever one had seen desperation in a face . . .

'Mind you, I was pretty certain of the way things

were shaping. As I said to you this morning, it was obvious that his associates . . . and all the while you were on the trail, my dear fellow – you had as good as got your hand on them! As a citizen of Lynton – not, perhaps, the least eminent . . .'

'We haven't arrested them yet, sir.' Gently was rude in his interruption. 'And as a matter of fact, it's not certain that they did it – the evidence we have can be construed either way.'

'But upon my word, Inspector—!'

Gently shut his ears to the man's expostulations. It was Fuller he was talking to, Fuller he wanted to goad. And the hunted look the miller was wearing was more eloquent than a dozen Pershores . . .

'But the whole trend of what the superintendent was telling me . . .'

Blacker had known something damning, it was too transparent.

'And at Newmarket anything can happen. From my own experience . . .'

Now Fuller was expecting his imminent arrest.

'Let's go into the office.'

'Eh?' Pershore broke off offendedly.

'I said let's go into the office. I want to talk to Mr Fuller.'

Protesting, the mayor-elect followed the two of them into the office. Fuller, walking unsteadily, led them into that part of it hidden from the road by the screen. His clerk made to rise from her typewriter, but Gently motioned her to remain.

'Don't go, Miss Playford . . . you may be able to help us. I dare say you have records of what occurred here last Thursday.'

'Last Thursday!' echoed Pershore. 'I fail to understand, Inspector.'

Gently shrugged. 'It's quite simple. I'm proposing to reconstruct the day of the crime.'

He got Pershore quiet at last, though wriggling with resentment. The second citizen of Lynton was alarmed by this fresh attack on his shining tenantry.

He took a seat in a corner from which he could command the proceedings, and seemed to be daring Gently to find one smutch on the miller's record.

To an unprejudiced eye the task could not have seemed a difficult one. Fuller, sitting slumped near the typewriter, had the appearance of being at the end of his tether. His clerk was looking shaken too. She kept darting agonized glances at her distressed employer.

In this connection, was it barely possible that Blacker's hint had been genuine . . . ?

'As far as you can remember it I want an account of Thursday the twelfth. Begin where you left home after breakfast, and continue to when you locked up to go to tea.'

'You can't expect . . . it's nearly a week ago . . .'

'So was the stag party – but you seem to have remembered that pretty well!'

About to say something, Fuller hesitated. Instead, he looked up at Gently with a wild appeal in his eyes.

Put him out of his misery – that was the message! He'd had as much as he could stand, and now he would welcome the inevitable touch on the shoulder . . .

'Go on – when did you leave the house?'

The relief of arrest was not coming yet.

Fuller's eyes sank again and his fists clenched tightly; when he spoke it was to the rough planks of the office floor.

'I . . . half past eight. That's my usual time. As far as I can remember I wasn't late that morning.'

'You drove straight to the mill?'

'Yes . . . no, I stopped to buy something. There was a milling article in *The Listener* – they mentioned it before the news.'

'Where did you buy it?'

'At Smith's in the Watergate.'

'Who did you talk to there?'

'Nobody . . . the assistant.'

'You spoke to nobody else on your way here?'

'No. I drove straight on to the mill.'

'Describe to me what happened directly after you arrived.'

'I – I parked my car outside.' Fuller sounded lost without the lead of interrogation. 'Mary showed me the mail . . . it was just the usual. Some invoices, receipts, an order from Bretts' – a stupid firm in Norchester wanting to sell me a cash-register. I told her what to get on with and then went into the mill.

'Two of the men were loading a lorry with the hoist – maize, supers, Kositos, the usual mixture for our

farmer customers. Two more were sacking flour . . .
Tom was minding the engine. The rest were putting
some oats through – later on it was English wheat.'

'You saw that all of them were at their jobs, did you?'

'Naturally – I go round every morning. And I check
stocks and keep an eye on the belting and machinery.'

'You noticed nothing out of the ordinary that
morning?'

'There was a slipping belt on one of the bolters . . .'

'What was Blacker doing, for instance?'

'Blacker . . .' Fuller's voice wavered. 'I don't particularly remember . . . he might have been helping to load.'

'How long were you in the mill?'

'An hour, the best part of. After that I checked the
loading on Bob Tillet's lorry . . . then one of my
customers came in to pay his bill, and another about a
wrong consignment. There's always plenty to do in the
office, with the phone ringing every five minutes.

'At one o'clock I went to lunch—'

'Just a minute! Who were those customers who came
in?'

Fuller gave a feeble shrug. 'One day is like another.
Mr Blakey from Torrington was one of them – then
there was a farmer called Howard, and the man from
Hillside Dairies. They were all customers – Mary can tell
you that.'

'What about Mr Blythely – didn't you see him that
morning?'

'I suppose so . . . yes, I did. I met him in the yard.'

'And you had a conversation?'

'I . . . not what you could call one.'

'What do you mean by that, Mr Fuller?'

'Well, we passed the time of day!'

'Hmn.' Gently's dissatisfaction was emphatic. 'Who else is there you've forgotten to mention? Take your time, Mr Fuller . . . we won't rush this memory of yours!'

'Excuse *me*, Chief Inspector!'

The mayor-elect was butting in.

'Since you've such a passion for the truth, however irrelevant it may seem—'

Wearily Gently fished out his pipe and stuck it into his mouth. Before long he was going to jump on this Lynton worthy, though it blighted the super's life from now until Christmas . . .

'Would you mind not interrupting, sir?'

'Interrupt, sir? I have something of importance to contribute!'

'I am endeavouring to conduct an enquiry—'

'And I, sir, am trying to assist you – however pointless your mode of proceeding appears to strike me!'

With an effort Gently held his peace. It was a long time since he had enjoyed the luxury of losing his temper officially. As a rule he suffered fools, if not gladly, at least intelligently . . .

'Very well, sir – provided it's relevant.'

'Thank you, Inspector. I feel sure you will think it so. The fact is that on Thursday last I paid a visit to the mill – though I am not surprised at my tenant having forgotten it, considering your hectoring treatment of him. Now why this should be—'

'At what time was that, sir?'

'Time?' Pershore snorted. 'I was in Lynton during the morning – naturally, I had no occasion to allot times to my movements. But if you will permit me to say so—'

'What was the purpose of your visit?'

'Eh?' Pershore's eyes opened wide. 'Do you dispute that this is my property? I came to view it, sir – I frequently overlook my investments! The keystone of success in business – and, speaking personally—'

'You went over the mill, did you?'

'And the bakehouse, since you are so precise.'

'Accompanied by Mr Fuller?'

'Certainly, as regards the mill.'

'Asking him questions, no doubt?'

'It has always been my unswerving policy—'

'So you were aware that the furthermost hopper contained spoiled flour?'

'That was something which I was unlikely to miss.'

Gently shook his head with monumental slowness.

'A little advice! Your position is ambiguous, if you don't mind my saying so. Your alibi is flimsy. You are apparently a frequenter of Newmarket. As the owner of this property, you will no doubt have some keys. And to cap it all, you admit knowing about the hopper of spoiled flour. Can't you see what the attitude of the average policeman would be?'

The mayor-elect's mouth opened incredulously.

'You can't be serious, Inspector!'

'I assure you I am, sir. You could quite easily become involved.'

'But I told you this morning—!'

'That you had not been in Lynton? I'm afraid we'd need witnesses to prove the truth of that.'

The great man of Lynton rocked slightly in his chair. Even Fuller had been roused from his apathy to stare at his landlord. As for the clerk, she seemed unable to believe her ears . . .

'So I would advise you to avoid drawing attention . . . if you value your civic reputation! Once the press get hold of these things they take a lot of living down. On the whole, the less your name appears in this business the better.'

It was a palpable threat, and Pershore was visibly shaken by it. An automatic protest died haplessly on his lips. One could have homicidal tenants – that was one thing! – but prospective mayors should not be personal participants . . .

'Of course, I – I see your point, Inspector!'

'Mmm.' Gently struck a match and set it to his pipe.

'It was never my intention – I think I know better—'

'If you don't mind I'd like to be getting on with my enquiry.'

Pershore lapsed into a dismal silence and Gently blew a number of smoke-rings. In the yard a lorry had drawn up, its idling motor providing an undertone to the beat of the naphtha engine.

Fuller, probably, should be out there giving the driver instructions.

'Why didn't you mention Mr Pershore's visit?'

'I'd forgotten about that.'

The miller sounded sullen, but somehow more composed. The Pershore interference had unfortunately given him time to pull himself together.

'It was quite a big thing to forget. Does Mr Pershore come round so often?'

'No, it isn't that – I'd just forgotten what day he came on.'

'But naturally, you remember it now?'

'He was here on Thursday morning.'

'At what time was that?'

'It was about eleven or just after.'

'What makes you so certain?'

'Mary fetches in the coffee about then, and she was out after it when Mr Pershore arrived.'

'What else have you forgotten?'

'Nothing . . . I've told you all I remember.'

Privately Gently was wishing Pershore would fry in hell for his self-consequential interruption. Fuller had been offered a breathing space, and his returning confidence showed what use he had made of it. If Blacker had talked, why was Gently going this devious way to work with the miller?

He couldn't have talked, and Fuller realized it . . .

'How long were you without a foreman?'

'How long? Roughly six or eight—'

'Quite a time in fact! Yet you suddenly appointed a new one.'

'It meant extra work . . .'

'Then why did you wait so long?'

'At first—'

'Meaning what?'

'The first week or two—'

'But you talked of six or eight weeks!'

'I know! It was later on—'

'So you were overworked for a month or six weeks, but did nothing about it till last Friday?'

'I'd been meaning to—'

'How long has Blacker worked here?'

'Several years – Mary will tell you—!'

'Six years. What about the others?'

'Of course, there's some of them—'

'Ten years? Twenty? One or two of them who worked here before you took the mill over?'

'Yes – one or two!'

'Then why was Blacker made foreman?'

'Because he's got the—'

'After a bare six years?'

'It's enough—'

'Over the heads of the others – and a man of his character?'

'I tell you—'

'Good for discipline, eh? Just the move to keep them happy!'

'I made him up on his ability!'

'About twelve hours after a murder on the premises!'

Pershore seemed about to break in again, but Gently nailed him down with a glance that made the mayor-elect shiver. Let him interfere this time – only let him dare! But Pershore had appreciated the threat of that glance . . .

'Why are you afraid of Blacker?'

'That's ridiculous . . .'

'Don't tell me you like the man!'

'We've always got on—'

'He's a bad lot, and you know it. He haunts the pubs and keeps company with prostitutes – probably runs one of them, if I know anything about it! And he's a slacker and a troublemaker, despised by the men you've put under him, on top of which he's insolent to you personally. If you're not afraid of him, why don't you kick him out? Of all the others, why make *that* fellow the foreman of your mill?'

'You don't know him, I tell you!'

'Oh, yes, I do – I've met Blackers before! They are constitutional parasites, Mr Fuller, one meets them at all levels. They are a work-shy race always on the lookout for the easy touch. And Blacker has found one in you, hasn't he? He's found a way of putting the pressure on! He saw something – he heard something – and now you're under his thumb.

'And that was on Thursday night, because he put the bite on you first thing on Friday morning.

'If it wasn't to do with Taylor, Mr Fuller, you'd better have a cast-iron story to tell!'

The miller shuddered as though he were being whipped, but the obstinate pout of his lips set tighter. Blacker hadn't talked, that was the sheet-anchor he was clinging to. Gently could suspect what he liked . . . but Blacker hadn't talked!

'Look – where did you see this before?'

Gently shoved the gold cross into the wretched man's hand.

'I – I haven't ever seen it!' Fuller shrank away from it sensibly. 'I don't understand—'

'And you wouldn't know where I found it?'

'No! How should I know?'

'Though it was amongst the barley-straw in the hay-loft?'

'I tell you – how should I know!'

This time the barb had caught something. Gently could feel the tug at his line. The desperation was seeping back into the miller's tone, a ghastly look had come into his eyes.

'Let me tell you something, Mr Fuller! We've got very comprehensive records of criminals like Taylor. He happened to have been a Roman Catholic – not a very good one, perhaps, but a man likely to have carried one of those things about.

'It could have been his – what have you got to say to that?'

'Nothing!'

'You mean it wasn't his?'

'I mean – no, I've never seen it before!'

'But even so, you've got an idea how it came to be in the loft – it was dropped in a struggle, wasn't it? Taylor's struggle for his life!'

The mixture of fear, despair and frustration in Fuller's look was difficult to analyse, but it was a long way from being the simple emotion of conscious guilt.

'You've got it wrong – he – he wouldn't have carried one!'

'Indeed? So you knew Taylor?'

'No! But a man like that – *he* wouldn't have been religious!'

'I disagree, Mr Fuller. Some crooks are very religious.'

The miller bit his lip and stared agitatedly at the floor. He seemed to be being wrenched by two contrary forces, two equal powers which prevented him from articulating.

'This cross . . . it might be anybody's . . . !'

Gently shrugged with expression.

'I mean . . . kids . . . a tramp – the door's never locked! Why imagine, for instance . . . it might have been there . . .'

'It's anybody's but Taylor's, in fact?'

'I didn't say that, but . . .'

'But you want to give that impression?'

'No – but why jump to the conclusion . . . ?'

Why indeed, when the miller had so unmistakably recognized the cross, and was trying his hardest to throw doubt on its ownership?

'Of course, it could have been dropped by the murderer.'

Gently took back the cross and held it poised in front of him.

'In strangling there's always a struggle – even when the victim is a small man! Unless you know precisely where to press – and Taylor's strangling was bungled – it takes an unexpected length of time to do a man in. Stranglers often panic and begin making mistakes . . .'

He had made a mistake himself. He had forgotten the presence of Miss Playford. The attractive clerk, the colour blanched from her cheeks, suddenly slipped forward from her chair and collapsed untidily on the floor.

'Inspector, that was completely uncalled for!'

Pershore was on his feet in a minute, spluttering his safely grounded indignation.

'You had no right, sir, whatever – your methods, if one may call them methods—!'

'All right – let's see to the lady!'

'But you had no right to employ such despicable—'

'For heaven's sake shut up – fetch some water, if you want to be useful!'

He was angry with Pershore and angry with himself. For the second time that afternoon he had slightly misplayed a promising card. Fuller was on his knees by his clerk, chafing her hands and murmuring reassuringly. Now the spell was broken – Gently had lost his opportunity!

'In spite of the threat you have seen fit to offer—'

'Take this glass, sir. There's a tap by the bakehouse.'

'At whatever personal risk, I feel bound in duty—'

'If you don't mind, we'll discuss it later.'

Pershore snatched the glass from him and stalked toweringly out of the office. Gently found a cushion and stuck it under Miss Playford's well-shod heels.

Twice in a row . . . it was too much of a bad thing! If he went on like this it was time for his retirement . . .

CHAPTER NINE

Fiery red sun had broken through slated sky, touching the teatime streets with rosiness. There was no warmth in the phenomenon. It made the east wind feel colder than ever. Like an inflamed and warning eye the sun peered down the comfortless streets, threatening to bring storm and wrack in its wake.

People were hurrying homeward, dour and silent as they had been all day. Along with the streets and buildings they seemed driven into themselves; nothing merged, nothing harmonized, everything was separate and alien to everything else.

Lynton . . .

'Just a coffee, please, waitress!'

Was it different in the summer? Perhaps . . . when the sun burned down! Or was it always like this, always at loggerheads with itself – was that the peculiar essence of the town?

'Do you belong to Lynton, miss?'

'Me? No, I come from outside.'

'Like it here, do you?'

'It's a bit slow, sometimes.'

'Ever think of moving?'

She hadn't, not really; but her young man was wanting to get a job in Cambridge . . .

Dutt had arrived, riding a massive constable's bike. He had parked it by the mill gate, in everybody's way, and was now leaning beside it and gazing absorbedly at the mill.

In the office, Pershore was haranguing his tenant. Gently had left him at it ten minutes ago. Miss Playford, feeling revived, had been sent home early, after resisting Fuller's offer to drive her in his car.

All the same, she'd been quite thrilled by his fuss when bringing her round.

Gently swallowed his coffee quickly, seeing Blythely enter the shop. The last card in his hand – and this one had to be played according to Hoyle!

They were checking up the till, he and his wife. The bread and rolls had all gone from the trays, the glass shelves in the windows carried little but soiled doyleys. Expert in everything appertaining to his trade, the baker could estimate his day's work to a few teacakes . . .

Gently put down a coin and took his hat. As he was crossing the street Mrs Blythely had advanced to drop the latch on the shop door.

'Just a minute – I want to come in!'

Her eyes met his through the glass, startled. Blythely, saying something, came over behind her, and with a pettish shrug she opened the door.

'Actually, we're closed, Inspector—'

The pettishness of the shrug found an echo in her voice. The shop, though empty, still smelled of cakes and pastries, while the air continued warm from the bakehouse round the corner.

'You can see what we've got left – there'll be nothing else till tomorrow.'

'I'm afraid I'm not here as a customer, Mrs Blythely.'

'Isn't it a bit late today? We're going to the pictures!'

'My regrets. I won't keep you longer than necessary.'

Blythely, out of his working togs, certainly seemed uncomfortably dressy. He was wearing a thick black suit of provincial cut, and a gold Albert peeped out of his waistcoat pocket.

'Like she says – it's a bit late. Can't you keep it for the morning?'

His glossy collar must have been purgatory to him.

'We don't often get out, and the wife looks forward to it – and what's more, you had all I can give you this morning.'

Gently shouldered the door closed and dropped the latch. What was it that made this uncouth man so impressive? A yokel, he looked, a country-town yokel, and yet – if Lynton really wanted a mayor . . .

'Shall we go upstairs?'

'What's wrong with the shop?'

'It's a little public, perhaps.'

'I've no business that can't be . . .'

'Possibly Mrs Blythely . . .'

'The same applies to her.'

Gently shrugged and found a bentwood chair for himself, reversing it in his customary manner. Mrs Blythely, sulky-faced, took possession of another, but her husband continued to stand under the fuse-boxes by the door.

'Now, about Thursday night . . .'

It was useless watching Blythely's expression. He only had one, and that was carved on his face as it might have been on oak.

'Some information has reached me which affects your statement.'

The eyes alone were changeable, but you only caught them in occasional, wary flashes.

'But first I want to ask you something which may seem a little personal . . . by the way, do you wear that watch-chain all the time?'

'Hmp!' Blythely grunted. 'I do – it was my father's.'

'Do you mind if I see it?'

Reluctantly the baker hooked his watch out of his pocket. The chain was a long one and opulently doubled. Besides the gold half-hunter there depended from it two seals and what appeared to be a masonic charm; they slowly revolved as Blythely held them suspended.

'Isn't there something missing from it?'

'Missing? What should be missing?'

'You take your religion seriously, Mr Blythely. Some people would carry a token of it.'

The quick eyes fell on him a moment, thrusting,

exploring. Then they returned to the watch with its little garnish of ornaments.

'We place no faith in graven images, if that's what you mean. They are the sign of the Whore and not of the Word which is Life.'

'I wasn't referring to graven images, just the token of your belief.'

'I have no token but the Word and the Hope in Jesu.'

'Not even one like this?'

Gently produced the gold cross.

'It seems to belong to that chain of yours, Mr Blythely . . . one would not be surprised to find it attached there.'

If the baker was unimpressible his wife was not. Her caught breath and instinctive gesture betrayed immediately her recognition of the object. But Blythely gave no sign. He merely reached out a clumsy hand for it.

'Where did you get this?'

'I'll tell you . . . does it happen to be yours?'

'I want to know where you found it.'

'First, I'd like you to answer my question.'

There was no rushing Blythely. He was like a pillar of insensible rock, standing there, feet planted, in his shapeless black suit. He had no handle, you felt, you could bring no pressure on him. It was like trying to manipulate one of the elements . . .

'Suppose it was mine, then?'

'In that case, when did you lose it?

'I didn't say it was mine – I said suppose.'

'You must answer me yes or no, Mr Blythely.'

'I do or I don't, but there's no must about it.'

Gently swung round to the baker's wife.

'Perhaps you can tell me, ma'am – remembering how quickly you recognized it!'

'I!' – she threw a helpless look at her husband – 'I don't know about it – it could be anybody's. There's nothing on it, is there . . . just a plain cross?'

'At least you *thought* you recognized it.'

'How could I, when there's nothing on it?'

'By being familiar with it, Mrs Blythely – as you would be if your husband wore it on his watch-chain!'

She shook her head stupidly and pretended to stare at the cross. Blythely was turning it about as though to make quite sure it carried no distinguishing marks.

'I can tell you it isn't mine.'

At last, a positive statement!

'My wife would be telling you a lie if she told you she had seen me wearing it.'

'And neither of you know to whom it belongs?'

'Like she says, there's nothing on it.'

'That's not quite the same thing, Mr Blythely.'

'You can't be sure with a thing like that.'

Prevarication, but not a lie – that was the baker's answer to an awkward question. It was a game which could go on all night, and probably never get him into a corner. And his wife, too . . . she had learned something of the gentle art!

'Very well – we'll leave it for the moment. It's something else which I came to see you about.'

Blythely handed back the cross and returned to his impassive stance by the door.

'You tell me you spent all the night in the bakehouse, the night of last Thursday and Friday. At the most you went out to the toilet – isn't that how the statement ran?'

'I said I went out to the toilet.'

'But you didn't go anywhere else?'

'I wouldn't have said I didn't.'

'All the same, you gave that impression!'

Blythely bowed his head slightly but made no other reply. At times one had the idea he was deaf, so little did anything said to him seem to register.

'As a matter of fact you did go somewhere else, didn't you? You were out of the bakehouse for an hour, between half past eleven and half past twelve. Before you deny it I should tell you that I have spoken to your assistant, and that the time has been established pretty exactly. Have you any comments to make, Mr Blythely?'

An expert in atmospheres, Gently was surprised by this one. To the closest observer the baker had provided no clue to the emotions which were governing him. Yet now there was something, and that something wasn't fear; suddenly, one was aware of a monumental agony.

'I wasn't going to deny it. What you say is the truth.'

The flat tone of the admission stung like a whiplash across the face.

'So you agree that you were absent—'

Gently broke off, catching sight of Mrs Blythely swaying ominously where she sat. Not another interruption like that – the first one had been costly enough!

He was really being dogged by the in-and-out propensities . . .

'I think your wife is feeling faint!'

Blythely didn't waste as much as a glance. More than ever he had the appearance of something carved from a block of wood.

'Your wife—' Gently got to his feet. Plainly he would have to be the one to render assistance. She was crouching now over her knees, her breath coming in gasps, but her husband was paying no more attention than if she had been in another world.

'Henry—!'

Was he deaf in fact?

'Henry – oh Henry, help me!'

She might as well have applied to the counter or the door.

Gently wavered, uncertain what to do. The baker's wife, though stricken, seemed to be in no danger of passing out, and he had an idea that she would resist if he offered her any aid . . .

'Mrs Blythely—'

'Henry!'

'This time there was panic in her voice, a sort of hysteric wildness.

'Henry, in God's name—!'

Now a flicker did pass over the averted countenance.

She burst into tears and sat hugging herself in a frenzy of abandonment. Out in the street they must have been able to hear her, because the passers-by began to stare through the big plate-glass windows.

'Henry – Henry!'

Could a stone have resisted that ring of desolation? But the baker never shifted, never changed his blank expression; less and less did he seem to be acting in the same scene.

Gently was frankly nonplussed. Between them, they had edged him quite out of it. From being a police interrogation the reins of which were in his hands it had developed into a domestic drama in which he was an embarrassed third party.

'Mrs Blythely – pull yourself together, ma'am!'

Regardless of him she sobbed and moaned.

'You – can't you do anything, instead of just standing there?'

He should have known it was pointless trying to bully Blythely.

Yet the affair had to be terminated somehow, if it were not to get out of hand. Already a group was collecting on the pavement beyond the window.

Quickly there would be others – and then, perhaps, a constable! In the end he would have to walk out and leave his most promising lead to grow cold . . .

'You're coming with me, the pair of you!'

He didn't stop to think what he would do if they resisted. Grabbing Blythely with one hand and snatching up his wife with the other, he propelled them through the shop and shoved them up the stairs beyond.

Muted by the plate glass, he heard the comment of the audience on this arbitrary curtain-pulling . . .

★ ★ ★

'Henry . . . forgive me, Henry!'

The actors had been moved, but the situation was continuing. Lit by the rosy sunset, Blythely's parlour had an angry, melodramatic appearance. It might have been a special stage-set for just such a scene as this.

Blythely, erect by the window, had his face darkened by the weird light behind him. On the dumpy settee Clara Blythely lay prostrate, by accident in a pose which would have pleased a producing eye.

'I'm so ashamed, Henry . . . so ashamed!'

Who could mistake the purport of the scene? It was classic in its simplicity, its principals were typecast. The pity of it was that Griffin wasn't here to enjoy the triumph of his acuteness.

'I was mad – you've got to believe me! I wasn't myself . . . it was somebody else!'

There was the Husband, there the Wife – hamming it, if anything; a good producer would have toned it down a little.

Wearily Gently seated himself and sought the consolation of his pipe. Had it been so simple, then, the crucial problem of Taylor's demise? The rest, that didn't concern him. It was a mystery, and it could stay so. *This* was the compass of the brief he held and here, apparently, the inconsequential answer!

Did it even matter who else knew what, guiltily or cunningly, according to their nature?

'You followed her out there, didn't you?'

On the screen of his mind he could project the whole picture, complete in time as in space.

'You saw them go in . . . you waited in the shadows. When she came out you let her go. To save her face—'

Mrs Blythely's tears came in a storm. She, at all events, was past equivocation. The baker, with head unbowed, still obstinately stared at nothing – yet he must have appreciated the endorsement given by his wife's lamentations.

'For him you couldn't wait. Once she was gone, you went in after him. Of course, he was unprepared, but even if he hadn't been—'

'I didn't go into the loft.'

It was the baker's first response for a good five minutes. His tone, like his expression, hadn't altered by one iota.

'Then how did this cross get there?'

'I told you it wasn't mine.'

'You mean that it belonged to Taylor?'

'How can one tell when there's nothing on it?'

The stupid repetition of this evasion irritated Gently. Surely by now the fellow could see . . . ! But a moment later his wife settled the question finally.

'It's mine . . . he gave it to me . . . oh God, it was a wedding present! Twenty years . . .'

Her tears smothered the rest.

'So – now we're getting somewhere!'

Gently took a long pull at his pipe.

'You jumped him as he came out, did you – took him completely by surprise! Did you know that we could tell that it was done from behind? But then you had to find a place for him, and not having much time—'

'I didn't kill that man.'

'Let me finish what I'm saying! Not having much time, you had to hide him about the premises – somewhere that was safe, with luck for a week or two. And what better place than that hopper of flour? Even the smell wouldn't notice very much! Furthermore, you might be able to fish him up later – if you could get him to the docks, an ebb tide would do the rest for you . . .'

'But I was not the one who killed him.'

'Listen – you can make a statement later! You had the keys in your pocket, didn't you? It was easy to slip in there. Taylor wasn't a heavy man, and you were strong and desperate. So up the steps he went on your back – one set, two sets, three sets, four sets: and then across the floor and into the hopper, where he disappeared as though he had never been.

'That was a bad moment – that was where you stopped to think! You wiped the sweat and listened to the silence, and you realized you had done what could never be undone.

'But Jimpson was in the bakehouse, already surprised by your absence – and what was more those buns had to be baked, if you were going to avoid comment. So down you went again, down those four sets of steps. The door was locked, you washed your hands, and all that remained was to get through the night – a task made the easier from having Jimpson to vent your nerves on!

'Can you deny on your oath that that's roughly what happened?'

The baker shook his head – a grand concession to

Gently's rhetoric! – and hesitated cautiously before he replied:

'I was hard on the boy – I've got to admit that. But all flesh is as grass when the Lord humbles our pride.'

'And that's all you've got to say?'

Gently felt like hitting him.

'Don't you realize where you stand – hasn't it penetrated at all?'

Apparently it hadn't. Blythely went on dumbly standing there. Like one of the grim flint towers of his native county, he was not to be moved by the storms that burst about his head.

On her settee his wife cried softly as though her grief were tiring itself out. She, too, seemed to have got into a world of her own, outside the influence of mere verbal formulae.

'I've tried to show you the construction—'

'I didn't kill that man.'

'But you were there at the time it happened . . . !'

'So you tell me, but I didn't see it.'

'Then you don't deny being there?'

'I haven't admitted it.'

'Following your wife to her rendezvous?'

'Has she said anything about a rendezvous?'

It was bordering on the farcical. In a moment, he would be denying that he had ever left the bakehouse. The effect of his prevarication was like that of a smokescreen, growing thicker and more confusing the further one pressed the pursuit.

'You, ma'am – *you* don't deny a rendezvous!'

Gently turned on the weaker vessel.

'You agree that the cross is yours – that ties you to the loft. And your conduct since you learned that your husband left the bakehouse leaves no doubt of a guilty secret – something you hoped he didn't know about!

'So perhaps *you* would like to be a little more articulate?'

Mrs Blythely moaned and covered her face, which certainly was not at its best just then.

'You don't have to get on to Clara.'

Blythely stirred from his monumental attitude.

'She can't tell you anything, so why upset her? It doesn't concern you – it lies between her and her Maker.'

His wife dropped her hands, as though unable to believe what she had heard. For a second or so she stared wildly at the baker, then she sprang up from the settee and threw herself sobbing on to his bosom. He made no move in recognition of her action.

'That's all very well—!'

'It doesn't concern you.'

'If you don't mind, I'll judge for myself!'

'Judge not lest ye be judged, says the Good Book.'

What the devil could one do? Gently had rarely been so baffled by the manoeuvres of an opponent. And in addition to his evasiveness the baker had a strange and formidable air of authority – when he made a statement it sounded, *ipso facto*, final.

'Go up to your room, Clara.'

Now he was even taking charge of the proceedings!

'The chief inspector and me've got a few things to talk over. You wait upstairs. I shan't be long.'

'Oh Henry . . . help me, Henry!'

'Go up to your room. Ask help of Him who has it in His Power.'

On the point of intervening, Gently decided to hold his peace. Running contra to the baker was a losing game, but if one gave him a good measure of rope, perhaps . . .

Mrs Blythely left the room without another word. The baker, as soon as the door closed, took a chair opposite to Gently and seated himself in his peculiarly stiff way.

'I haven't much to tell you, but it may be of some use.'

The foxy eyes rested upon him steadily for a moment.

'But first I say to you, meddle not with the Lord's business. He has seen fit to lay a burden on two of His children, and neither you nor any man has the right to increase that burden. Revenge is Mine, saith the Lord, it belongeth to no man.'

'At the same time, Mr Blythely—'

'I will hear no worldly equivocations.'

Gently gave him a long look before silently shrugging.

'For the rest, I don't mind helping you as far as I can. It's true that I was round the back watching the stable.'

'You followed your wife?'

'If she had gone there I may have done.'

'Please, Mr Blythely!'

'It's true that I watched the stable.'

Gently heaved a deep sigh. 'Very well – you watched the stable!'

The baker nodded impassively, well aware of the points he was scoring.

'You've seen that convenience there? I was standing inside it. In there you can see the stable, though you can't see the yard. Well, I heard several people go by during the time I was in there – two of them met in the passage and had a few words together.'

'What did they say?'

'I wasn't able to hear. And another thing, I don't remember hearing them go away again. But just after that somebody else came down the yard. He stopped a bit in the passage and then came back again in a hurry.'

'How do you mean – in a hurry?'

'It sounded as though he was running.'

'Was anyone chasing him?'

'I only heard the one. Then ten minutes later there were steps from the passage again. Somebody went up and out of the yard, and that's all I remember hearing.'

'And Taylor – what about him?'

'I told you, I couldn't see anyone.'

'Not entering or leaving the stable?'

'I never set eyes on Taylor.'

Half an hour later Gently was out in the street with precisely that information and no more. The most his arts had availed him was to get a rough sort of time-table, as inaccurate, probably, as these things usually were.

And how much could he believe, of all that puzzling interview? Was it in good faith, or partly so, or had even Clara Blythely's act been an inspired piece of misdirection?

He shook his head at the sunset-outlined building as he turned away towards the town. His third card had gone, not unprofitably, it was true, but the trick he had won was perhaps more tantalizing than the two which had just escaped him.

Griffin, he was sure, would have clapped the baker behind bars directly . . .

CHAPTER TEN

GENTLY SLEPT BADLY that night in spite of the blandishments of the sprung mattress with which the management of the St George had furnished him. He couldn't get the baker out of his mind. The wretched fellow haunted his dreams all night long. Now he would wake up arguing with him, chewing away desperately at some perfectly obvious proposition which Blythely was simply staring out of existence; now the situation appeared in symbols, with Blythely as a towering cliff and Gently's logic the waves beating helplessly against it.

The baker had got the better of him, that was the whole trouble. For once in a way he had met somebody who was a match for him. He had never got hold of the initiative. It had always lain with Blythely. The baker's wife had given Gently weapons, but they had glanced aside from her husband's head. Blythely had told him just as much as he wanted to, no more and no less, and the defeat rankled in a thousand uneasy images.

Because, after all, hadn't Gently pierced the defences of a score of antagonists more redoubtable than this small-town provincial tradesman? Professionals, some of them had been! – men who had known every twist and pressure of the interrogator's art.

Yet here he had been checkmated, firmly and unhesitatingly.

The baker was wearing an armour more impregnable than guile.

A clatter of bells penetrated the troubled caverns of his sleep, shattering, insistent, not to be denied. Gently groaned and opened his eyes. The telephone on his bedside table was ringing. A grey, unfriendly light suggested that the hour was unseasonable. He couldn't quite see whether his watch pointed to five or six.

'Yes . . . Chief Inspector Gently?'

In the courtyard below his window somebody was having trouble starting a car.

'Inspector Griffin here . . . sorry to wake you up. We think we've got a line on one of those two men.'

'Ames and Roscoe, you mean?'

Gently sat up with a rush.

'Yes, but he's dead. The county police have pulled him out of the river a couple of miles upstream. They think he's Ames and we're sending our print man. I thought you'd like to get out straight away.'

He could see his watch now. It was seven minutes past five. The car outside was firing jerkily, probably on only three cylinders.

'What happened . . . how did he die?'

'They think he was stabbed.'

'Send round for me, will you? I'll be ready in five minutes.'

Automatically he dropped the receiver and began feeling for his clothes. Another one of that fated trio – dead, and making sixes and sevens!

For the moment he couldn't react to the information, it was so unexpected and cataclysmic. He pulled on his clothes stupidly, entirely forgetting his collar and tie.

Down below he found a sleepy-eyed maid and got from her a strong, sweet cup of tea. The refractory car, an ancient Morris, got going just in time to make an incoming police Wolseley pull up with a squeak of tyres.

Gently was never at his best at that hour in the morning. Now, huddled into his clothes without washing or shaving, he felt somehow out of things, as though he were being dragged along as a spectator.

Griffin, on the other hand, was looking particularly smart and sharp. He had both washed and shaved and his hair was sleek with brilliantine smelling of eau de Cologne. Also, he was wearing a clean shirt. Out in the country, Gently had to make a shirt go a couple of days.

'I was riding on my beat from Cuffley to Morton, taking in Long Lane and Five Mile Drain.'

The constable who had landed the body was young and hard-eyed. He was obviously enjoying being the centre of attraction.

'I arrived here at the sluice at three minutes to three a.m., when I was accosted by William Harmer, by profession a drainage maintenance inspector. He informed me as how he was making his customary round when he caught sight of something white down in the water by the sluice-gate. On directing his torch upon this object he came to the conclusion that it was a human body . . .'

If it was bleak and dismal now, at half past five, what had it been like at three minutes to three o'clock! The rain was spitting on the slow-flowing surface of the wide, muddy stream and darkening the brickwork of the lonely little pump-house.

Across the marshes one could just see Lynton, a gloomy stain against the reluctantly lightening sky. Apart from this nothing broke the monotonous flatness except the river reaches and the improbable straightness of the drain. Drawn to infinity, it exercised a curious fascination on the eye.

But at three minutes to three one wouldn't have seen much of that . . .

'I approached the sluice-gate and looked where Harmer showed me. Being in no doubt that it was a human body, I requested Harmer to fetch the grapnels which are kept in the pump-house, and with his assistance embarked in the rowing-boat which is moored here.'

It was still moored there, in the relief channel beside the sluice. A weathered double-ender, it could have done with a bail with the chipped enamel saucepan lying in the bows.

'After several attempts we succeeded in catching hold

145

of its shirt and getting it up into the boat. Leaving Harmer in charge of it, I proceeded to the nearest telephone at Coldharbour Farm and reported the occurrence.'

That was all, in official parlance, but one could easily imagine the rest. It had been raining steadily at three o'clock and the constable was probably wet through. And how long had Harmer had to wait with the corpse at that desolate spot, smoking perhaps, watching eagerly for a light on the lonely fen lane?

Gently glanced towards him with curiosity. A tough, leathery-looking little marshman, he had probably been on these vigils before . . .

The Lynton police surgeon came out of the pump-house where the corpse had been deposited.

'He was stabbed all right – a proper amateur's job. Sixteen stab-wounds scattered about the left side of the back and three ribs fractured. Only about two of the stabs would have done for him directly. Nothing elsewhere and there doesn't seem to have been a fight.'

'When was he killed?'

'Not long ago, taking into account the low temperature of the water. About midnight, I'd say, or a little before.'

'What about the weapon?'

The police surgeon shrugged.

'I'll tell you more about that after I've had him on the slab. Guessing roughly, I'd say it was an ordinary sheath knife. The blade would be about an inch in width.'

Gently was asking the questions, but he couldn't get

146

rid of the feeling that he was somehow supernumerary. If only he'd remembered to put on his collar and tie! Of the group on the riverbank he felt nearest akin to Harmer. The marshman, sopping wet in a shapeless old coat of Derby tweed, looked as though he had never been near a collar and tie in his life.

'We'd better take a look at his clothes.'

They followed him into the pump-house. Inside there was very little room, except that taken up by the machinery. A couple of hurricane lamps, impressed from the farm, were beginning to grow pale in the dull light of day.

The body lay on the floor, a tarpaulin sheet pulled over it. A pile of clothing beside it consisted only of trousers, shirt and underclothes. Gently stirred them up disinterestedly.

'New – no markings. Was there anything in the pockets?'

One of them was turned inside out, and a frayed edge showed where a maker's label had been torn away. The shirt was of a popular make which might have been bought anywhere.

'That ties it in.'

Griffin pointed to the frayed edge.

'The labels were torn off Taylor's clothes, too. You can see how it works. This bloke was too big to strangle, so chummy took a knife to him.'

'And he wasn't an expert with that, either.'

Nevertheless he had done his job with it, stabbing frantically till his victim collapsed. And then, coolly enough, he had sought to conceal the identity . . . naïvely, perhaps, but efficiently as far as it went.

Griffin's print-merchant got up laboriously from a corner where, by the aid of a powerful torch, he had been making a rough check.

'It's him all right . . .'

Gently, after a glance under the tarpaulin, had never been in doubt. There was no mistaking the ex-pug's battered features, which sported three separate scars in any case.

But if only they could have got to him six hours sooner!

'How long has the tide been ebbing?'

He turned to Harmer.

'Set in near midnight, I shouldn't wonder.'

'How fast does it run?'

''Bout four or five here. Farther up it's slower.'

'Anyone got a map?'

Somebody fetched a one-inch Ordnance Survey from the locker of one of the cars and Gently spread it out over a convenient part of the machinery. Griffin handed him a hurricane lamp, though it wasn't strictly necessary.

'Ten or twelve miles . . . less, probably, since it wasn't floating. This is your district – have you got any ideas about it?'

Griffin examined the map keenly, not to be rushed into a hasty judgment. One idea was as good as another, but Gently felt somehow compelled to defer to the spruce inspector.

'There's not much up that way for miles. It's all fen and grazing marshes till you get to Beetley.'

A glance could tell you that.

'But there's the main south road there – that runs close to the river near Apton. And there's a lane down here to one of the old drainage mills.'

'Let's get down there and see if we can find anything.'

It was going to be a wet day. Already the interval of spitting was over and the rain reverting to a steady, measured rhythm. It hissed in the wheels of the Wolseley as it sped along the level highway, rising in sheets where puddles had collected.

Over the low hedges, comfortless in their early green, one saw sodden fields of black fen soil. Now and then, appearing like ships, were great barns or farmhouses in the rusty Northshire brick and pantile, by each a leafing elder or two.

Westward lay the marshes and the river, low, waterlogged, the primeval haunt of every depressing tone of brown, green and grey.

'It's got rid of the wind, anyway.'

Griffin wanted to talk – no doubt he'd already got a theory. Gently, sitting hunched over his first pipe of the day, was thinking more in terms of a roadhouse where one might get a sandwich and a cup of coffee.

'Doesn't seem as though they got far, does it?'

Somebody had to make that remark!

'Looks as though they got out of town to give us the slip, and then hung around still trying to get whatever it was . . .'

'And now there's only one left alive.'

'You think chummy will go after him too?'

Gently grunted.

'Ask yourself the question! If it was necessary to get rid of two of them, it must be necessary to get rid of the other one. And they couldn't all be making love to Mrs Blythely in the hayloft.'

Griffin was silent for a few moments after this rebuff. He had an irritating way of looking injured, Gently noticed. Beyond the streaming windows a dyke-wall had risen to conceal the view to the right. Judging from what they had passed already, there was small prospect of the coffee and sandwiches materializing.

'It must be something in Lynton they were after, though.'

One day, would someone tell Griffin he was commonplace?

'And it has to be pretty big – what happened to Taylor didn't shake them off. Chummy meant business, but they were still trying for the jackpot.'

'Almost looks like a racket again, doesn't it?'

'If I didn't know Lynton . . .'

'Look – isn't that a café we're coming to?'

Griffin must have breakfasted already, because he didn't join Gently in his hasty snack. Instead, he remained in the back of the car, his eyes fixed on the road along which they ought to have been travelling.

'If there's traces of blood – in this rain . . .'

Gently got back beside him feeling a little more benevolent. The coffee had been freshly ground, and scalding hot at that. As well as two sandwiches he had gobbled down a Chelsea bun.

'Five minutes won't matter after all the rain we've had.'

'I was thinking of footprints, too.'

'The same applies to them.'

It wasn't much further to the road-section near Apton. In the distance one could see the circular brick tower of the old drainage mill, capless and sailless but firmly lined in the dirty sky.

The lane leading to it was narrow but kept in good repair; though the mill was disused, it probably stood at an important point in the current drainage system.

'If it had been dry we might have seen car-tracks.'

It wasn't dry, so what was the point of harping on it? This wasn't the first time rain had assisted a criminal . . .

The lane ended indefinitely by a clump of bush alders. Griffin, springing out almost before the car stopped, led the way past them to the riverbank beyond.

It was a spot quite as desolate and depressing as the sluice they had lately visited. The mill-tower, seen close-to, looked paltry and devoid of interest. A gap had been rent in the fabric above the door, apparently with intention, while the interior seemed to have been devoted to purposes unspecified.

'Fishermen . . .'

Griffin sniffed but didn't pursue his researches. The litter of paper about the earthy floor was patently of earlier date than yesterday.

'Is the fishing good in these parts?'

'Ask Worsnop there.'

'We get some good bream, sir,' put in the constable in question. 'One of the blokes in my club pulled out a nine-pounder on a number twelve . . .'

Beside the mill still remained the axle of its paddle-wheel, but the wheel itself had long since vanished. The apron of turf stretching to the river was tough and springy. It bore a number of marks, but they were shallow and indefinite. If there had been any blood it would have been washed out several hours ago.

'Not much to see here.'

Griffin sounded disappointed.

'I could have sworn it was the spot – it's the only likely place. Do you think we can be certain about the distance the body travelled?'

Gently plodded down the bank and stood gazing into the muddy water. The tide was beginning to make again, but the level of the water hadn't sensibly risen. On the other bank a bed of soiled reeds showed that it had some two or three feet to go.

'He might have thrown the clothes in his car and got rid of them anywhere . . .'

'Ames's clothes, you mean?'

'Mmn. But Ames had to get here . . . isn't it three miles to Apton? There's just a chance he pinched a bike – what do you think of that?'

Griffin stared at him seriously, trying to follow the logic of it.

'Suppose chummy brought him here . . .'

'It isn't such a helpful supposition.'

'But until we find a bike . . .'

'There's one down there in the bed of the river.'

He went back into the car and smoked while Worsnop waded for the abandoned bicycle. The rain had taken another turn for the worse and was beating like rods on the Wolseley's roof and bonnet. Inside the car smelt dankly of moist leather, while a trickle of water was finding its way through one of the door jambs.

Griffin and Worsnop, reappearing with the bicycle, looked as though they had relinquished all hopes of staying dry.

'It's a Raleigh, nearly new – dynohub lighting and everything.'

'Nobody was going to throw that in the river.'

'What shall we do – issue a description?'

'First we'll take it into Apton and see if anyone's lost one.'

He was feeling more himself now, wreathed in a cloud of navy cut. That little bit of luck with the bicycle had offset the initial disadvantage of being dragged out of bed . . . besides, Griffin was in something of a pickle now, himself! He had got all over mud helping to strap the bicycle to the roof rack.

One piece of luck sometimes led to another, and Gently's seemed to be temporarily in form. At Apton the constable was out on his beat, but his wife, a buxom matron with a lively eye, had just booked the very piece of information they were after.

'Fred Larkin's just been round here . . . somebody pinched his bike from outside the village hall last night.'

'Did he leave a description?'

'It's a green Raleigh roadster, newish, frame number – where's the book! – PYS7 stroke 2964. Got a lot of extras on it, he says, and he only bought it in January.'

'Where can we find him?'

'He works in the garage – but won't you have a cuppa? I've got the pot on for my husband, and you look as though you could stand one.'

In spite of a disapproving Griffin, Gently accepted the invitation. The Apton Constable's kitchen was a cheerful place and his wife a comfortable body. Not knowing who he was, she at once placed Gently as the one in charge of whatever was afoot.

'Have you any strangers staying in the village?'

'There's the vicar's nephew, who's a bit of a lad. Down from Cambridge, he is.'

'Nobody at the pub?'

'They sometimes have a commercial.'

'What buses come to the village?'

'There's Service 56, runs between Westwold and Lynton.'

'What time was the last bus through yesterday?'

'I'll have to look it up. It's going to Lynton and gets in here at something to eleven. Do you reckon it was someone off the bus who whipped Fred Larkin's bike?'

The village was typical of that part of the county, a short, level street winding between a huddle of quite spacious houses, several with architectural pretensions. In the centre it broadened into a small plain where grew a massive oak tree. Here there was a shop and post office, and around the corner a garage with a solitary petrol pump.

Griffin followed Gently doggedly as he strolled into the latter.

'Is there a Fred Larkin here?'

A figure in soiled dungarees eased itself from under a pre-war Singer which almost filled the small building.

'I'm a police officer . . . I understand you had your bicycle stolen last night.'

He was a young fellow with ginger hair, obviously alarmed by this unnatural incursion of policemen.

'I . . . yes – somebody took it.'

'Would you like to repeat the registration number?'

He was so upset that he had to have two goes at it.

The village hall was a rather ornate structure of red brick and stone, incorporating also the village's two war memorials. On the noticeboard was still pinned a weird amateur poster advertising in brushwork last night's 'Gala Supper Dance'; in a cycle stand beside it three machines had been left.

'I put it there, three from the end . . . there was two other blokes with me.'

'What time was that?'

'About eight . . . you see, my girlfriend . . .'

'Was that the last time you saw it?'

'I'm going to tell you – she wasn't ready! I went up for her, and . . . one thing and another . . . it was getting on for ten, and the bike was here then.'

'When did you miss it, then?'

'When I came out. I thought someone had shifted it

for a joke. When it wasn't here this morning, I went to the police.'

'Where's the bus stop?'

'It's over there by the oak.'

He hung around uncomfortably, probably under the impression that he was going to get his bicycle back. Gently ignored him and went over to the post office. There, in a red frame, were posted the times of the village's rather infrequent bus service. There was nothing in the evening between 7.10 and 10.42.

'We'll want a list of all these villages covered by Service 56 – the ones that use it as well as the ones it goes through. Better phone in to H.Q. and get them on the job. I want the check-up before the evening paper gets around.'

'You think they were biding out there?'

Even Griffin was beginning to be impressed by the breaks Gently was getting.

'I think it's worth a try – and we may be lucky. Though if Roscoe's got any brains he won't be waiting for the evening papers.'

'He might be thinking that Ames—'

'That's why I want a quick check-up.'

Again he got back into the car and left Griffin to deal with the donkey work. Now he was almost truculent – damnation, he wasn't in the Central Office for nothing!

Larkin, still wandering like a ghost, seemed fascinated by the sight of his bicycle strapped to the roof of the car. It wasn't until Griffin came back from the phone box

CHAPTER ELEVEN

I T WAS STRAIGHT, steep, regular, rhythmic Northshire rain, which, having struck its tempo, seemed intending to continue till the crack of doom.

The market square, its gutters rushing with water, was as empty as a hosed-out fish barrel. In the streets one met only a few housewives hastening between the shops, their brightly coloured plastic macs glistening under advanced umbrellas.

It was dark, too. The shops had on all the lights in their display windows, usually switched off during the day. Near St Margaret's Church, where there were no shops worth speaking of, a murky gloom seemed to have settled among the buildings.

As for the pigeons . . . who knew where they went on a day like this? Probably they had long since congregated in Fuller's mill, taking charge of one forgotten corner or another.

Gently, who could rarely be bothered with such things, had been obliged to accept the offer of a car.

It had stood most of the morning among the puddles in the mill yard, getting in the way of the lorries which came in for loading.

Then it had disappeared, not long before lunch, going back in the town direction. Fuller from his office and Blythely from his shop had both watched it departing – the one *con espressione* and the other with none at all.

And still it had rained and rained and rained; you couldn't shift a yard without huddling into a raincoat and doing up every button.

The sky, a smoky wrack, seemed to rest on the gleaming rooftops. Some of the storm drains had got blocked with rubbish and were spreading aprons of water which they should have carried away.

Going in for lunch, grumpy and depressed, Gently had been obliged to change his shoes, socks, and trousers. He hated the rain, even of any kind, and this bout looked like being the limit.

'It's those atom bombs what's doing it!'

He had exchanged a word or two with the maid who had taken away his discarded clothing to be dried. Logically speaking and according to the scientists . . . but had they really had such filthy weather in those halcyon days before the Second World War?

Before lunch he went into the bar and warmed himself with a hot rum. From the menu he chose the most solid-sounding dishes, beefsteak pudding followed by treacle tart and custard. Then he topped it all off by having a liqueur with his coffee, and had ordered an expensive cigar to be brought to him.

'Have you got anything yet?'

There had been singularly little news from head-quarters. He had phoned them twice while he had been at the mill.

'There's been two more reports in . . . both negative, I'm afraid.'

Could he have been wrong all along the line about that confounded bicycle?

His morning's work had done nothing to clarify the situation. He could almost have predicted the result in advance. Fuller had an alibi which checked where it touched – he'd taken a van into Cambridge to pick up some spare parts. But Blythely! – well, he was running true to form. If it was a lie it was such a thin one that it almost compelled belief.

'Don't you remember my wife telling you we were going to the pictures?'

Likely, that, wasn't it – after the emotional crisis Gently had provoked by his visit!

But the baker had stuck to the story, even elaborating it a little. And Mrs Blythely, whom Gently had cornered on her own, sullenly agreed that they had gone to the Ambassador.

'Very well – describe the programme,' Gently had challenged the pair of them.

Mrs Blythely had made a fair hand of it, her husband had been vaguer. And neither of them could remember meeting anyone they knew. Once again, by using sheer dead weight, as it were, the baker had shouldered Gently aside . . .

'How about that bike – aren't they through going over it yet?'

'We've only just got Larkin's prints back, and being in the river . . .'

'There'll have been grease on the frame.'

'He seems to have kept it washed down with petrol.'

'That's a damn silly thing to do! What about the lot who're dragging the river?'

'They rang up half an hour ago and we sent out some thermoses of hot soup.'

He hung up impatiently and dragged at his cigar, which tasted damp. All the leads he'd got his hands on seemed to be frittering themselves away. In the lunchtime paper had appeared a chaste paragraph about a body taken from the river, and if Roscoe hadn't skipped already, then he would as soon as his eye fell on that.

Meanwhile this rain, boring down like the commencement of some fresh deluge . . .

'Do you reckon these could be something, sir?'

Dutt, coming in on his lunch relief, found Gently still brooding by the phone. The cockney sergeant's boots were squelching and his clothes sagged wetly, but nothing could quite upset the chirpiness of his manner.

'Have you come into money, Dutt?'

It was a pad of fivers that was proffered to him.

'I've only got it official, sir, pending what you thinks about it.'

'Where did you pick this up?'

'At the Central Garage, sir. This Blacker goes in there just now and buys himself a brand new motor scooter, and being as we're so interested, I thought I'd take charge of the lolly.'

'A motor scooter!' Gently whistled. 'That's quite an item to be paying cash for.'

'Yessir. And those notes is new ones – got the same letters, one or two of them.'

Always it seemed to come out of the clouds, but always you had had to work for it. This time he had been squandering Dutt on what seemed a pointless tailing stint, and now, when he was stuck for a move . . .

'Get some dry clothes on and have your lunch, Dutt. I'll take these round personally.'

'Yessir. And do I go on tailing him?'

'No – I've got a hunch that we've got what you were after!'

Abandoning the cigar, he set off on his tour of the banks. It wasn't a long job in Lynton, where the principal branches were grouped together in streets near the market square. At the third one he made the contact he was looking for.

'Four of these notes were paid out by us recently. We probably issued the others also, but we haven't got a definite record.'

'Who did you pay them to?'

'Would you mind stepping into the manager's office?'

The manager was a spare, gaunt-faced individual with cropped grey hair and tired-looking eyes. He seemed a little put out by Gently's request.

'I suppose it is absolutely essential, Inspector . . . ?'

'You are aware that I am investigating a homicide.'

'At the same time, we try to guard the interests of our clients . . . publicity, in this case, could be cruelly damaging.'

'Unless the party is implicated there should be no publicity.'

'That's out of the question! He's our largest private depositor. After twenty years with us I think I can answer for his character. In Lynton his reputation is of the highest.'

'The less he has to fear, then, from an enquiry of this sort.'

The manager frowned at the documents which lay on his blotter. Plainly, he would like to have given Gently a flat refusal. Homicide was a phrase to toy with, certainly, but when it came to annoying his largest private depositor . . .

'The notes in question formed part of a substantial withdrawal. They were collected by our client in person at rather short notice, though of course we were happy to oblige.'

'How much exactly?'

'Ten thousand pounds.'

'When were they collected?'

'On the twelfth, following notice on the eleventh.'

'Is it usual for him to withdraw large sums in cash?'

'Once or twice, it might be . . . I would have to examine the back records, perhaps correspond with headquarters.'

'When was the last such withdrawal?'

'I'm afraid I must have notice of that question.'

'Let me know as soon as you can, please. And the name and address of this client?'

The manager sighed and gestured helplessly with his narrow shoulders.

'It is Geoffrey Pershore, Esq., of Prideaux Manor, Prideaux St John. And may I beg, on his behalf, that this matter is withheld from the press?'

But Gently had already taken his hat.

The maid who let him in was a country girl with chubby dimpling features. She left him standing in the lofty but austere hall with its graceful painted stairway at the side.

Coming up the drive, Prideaux Manor had looked a rather chill and forbidding place. The blank, white Regency front with its double row of tall windows struck a desolate note among the dripping and leafless elms.

Seen at closer quarters it was more friendly. The windows came to life, there was warmth in the ornate stone porch; a comfortable proportion established itself among the rectangles which, at a distance, seemed dreary.

Now, inside, one was obliged to acknowledge a graciousness about the house. The stairway alone was a gem of airy elegance. Lit by a high, round-topped window, the hall had a chapel-like atmosphere of peace. The chequered tiles of the floor had not been covered, a solitary bust in a niche gave point to the wall facing the stairs.

'Will you come this way?'

The maid led him along a white-panelled corridor on the walls of which hung a number of flower paintings in oil. At the end of it he was ushered through the door of a small, period-furnished drawing room.

'Ah, good day, Inspector!'

Pershore was waiting for him by the hearth, in which a brisk fire was burning. Legs astride, he might have been consciously studying the part of a landed proprietor at home. To his right was a low table bearing a decanter of whisky and an open box of cigars. He was smoking one of the latter, and a half-empty glass stood by the carriage clock on the mantelpiece behind him.

'What a day we've been having . . . !'

His tone of genial patronage completed the picture.

'Won't you give Grace your coat? After your drive, a little whisky . . .'

Gently allowed himself to be discommoded of his hat and coat and seated himself carefully on an inlaid Sheraton chair. The room was all of a piece, all strictly Regency. One picture was certainly a Constable, another probably a Crome . . .

Was it Pershore himself who somehow struck a false note?

'You have some news for me, Inspector?'

'There have been some developments.'

'Ah! I am glad to hear that.'

'You may be able to help me with some information.'

Savouring his cigar smoke, Pershore looked pleased. This was treating him as he deserved – Mahomet had

166

come to the mountain! He gestured gracefully towards the cigar box, but Gently shook his head.

'As you are aware, in my opinion—'

'Do you live here alone, Mr Pershore?'

'I? I am married, Inspector! My wife is the noted horsewoman—'

'Is she at home at present?'

'She is touring America with the English team.'

'Your domestic servants?'

'I have three – but really—!'

'Forgive me for asking personal questions.'

The mayor-elect was not so pleased now. His watery blue eyes regarded Gently suspiciously. What was he getting at, this disrespectful fellow? From the first he had made some quite unwarrantable suggestions . . .

'Some bank notes have come into our possession.'

'Indeed?'

Pershore made the retort sound withering.

'We have succeeded in tracing four of them. They were issued by the Lynton branch of the National Provincial. It appears that they were paid out to you, sir.'

'That is not improbable, since I have always banked there.'

'As part of a rather large sum.'

'I am not a pauper, Inspector.'

'At a recent withdrawal. In point of fact, last Thursday.'

His rage was beginning to simmer, you could see it welling up visibly. His fleshy cheeks had turned quite livid, his lips were quivering. For a moment he was at a loss to find a suitable expression for his anger.

'In the first place, Inspector, this is none of your business—'

'Under the circumstances, sir—'

'Under no conceivable circumstances! What I do with my money concerns nobody but myself – I pay my tax, and there is an end of it!'

'Nevertheless, on this occasion—'

'On this occasion you are a fool, Inspector.'

'I require to know to whom you paid that money.'

'And the answer is simple – I haven't paid it!'

If he had hoped to dumbfound Gently by this riposte he had entirely succeeded. It was the one answer which the other had not been expecting, and sheer surprise kept him momentarily silent. Pershore, glaring fiercely at him, picked up his glass and gulped down the rest of the whisky.

'No, sir, I haven't paid it – how does that square with your pryings and ferretings?'

'You are positive of that?'

'As positive as a man can be of his private affairs.'

'The bank can hardly have made a mistake . . .'

'On the contrary, Inspector, it seems to have made two – and as a net result it is losing my account!'

Gently stared uncomprehendingly at the circular period grate. This wasn't the way it should have gone, at all! An error might have been made in checking the serial number of a single note, but four, selected from thirty-odd others . . . how was it possible to make mistakes of that sort?

'You'd better have the whole story, since you're so interested in my business!'

Pershore was ugly in his triumph and eager to rub it in.

'No doubt you don't have much to do with people who have large sums at their command. From your handling of this case, Inspector, I should say that you still have a great deal to learn.'

Could Pershore be lying, so stupidly certain as he seemed of himself?

'You must know that I am the Commodore of the Lynton Yacht Club – a distinction, I may say, not entirely unearned. We hold regattas on the river – I, myself, own the flagship. But now we are thinking of extending our activities.'

'Regarding the money—'

'You will listen to me, Inspector! You came here with a certain question, and now you will listen to the answer.

'We are forming a cruising section – you understand what that means? Those of us with means are purchasing yachts for sea-going . . .'

Underlying the bluster, couldn't one catch the uneasiness, the lived-down fears of a nobody become somebody? That cultivated accent – what was the burr behind it? Now and then, when he was excited, it slipped out tantalizingly. You could be sure of one thing: Pershore wasn't bred in Northshire . . .

'Stanhope got in ahead of me, but he made a bad mistake. The old fool who owned the *Natalie* wouldn't take a cheque for the money. Immediately I got in touch—'

'Don't you come from the West Country?'

'What?'

'Gloucestershire . . . perhaps Somerset way?'

Pershore froze in the posture he had adopted, his cigar raised to make a point.

'What has that got to do with it?'

'Nothing. I was simply curious.'

'Why should you be curious about that?'

'It's a way policemen have.'

Pershore gave him several odd little glances. He seemed thrown out of his stride by this irrelevant enquiry. But finally he flicked the ash from his cigar and went on with his lecture.

'As I was saying, I got in touch with my bank for a short-notice withdrawal of the requisite sum. In the meantime I sent this Upcher a telegram – unfortunately, he wasn't on the telephone . . .'

Was it imagination, or had some of the bounce gone out of him? Occasionally, now, he fumbled for a word.

'On Thursday I collected the money and sent a further telegram announcing my intention . . . I was just about to set out for Starmouth when Upcher rang me up.

'In spite of my telegram he had sold the *Natalie*! It appears that a third party was interested and took him the money on Wednesday evening.

'Thus you have your answer, Inspector. You know for what the money was intended and that it has never been out of my hands. Am I wrong in supposing that an apology from you would not be out of place?'

'Hmn.' Gently shrugged towards the grate. 'And the address of this Upcher fellow?'

'Naturally I will supply you with it. Stanhope, if you intend to persist with this enquiry, you can get in touch with at his offices in Ely Street.'

'Where's the money now?'

'Here in this house. I have a built-in safe.'

'Shouldn't we just take a look at it?'

'If you insist – but under protest.'

To rub in the protest he remained straddling the hearth for a few seconds. Then, without deigning to toss Gently another word, he strode magnificently towards the door.

The safe was in a book-lined study at the other end of the corridor. A false front of books was intended to conceal it, but the facetious titlings on the spines gave away the secret at once to those familiar with such contraptions. A big Chubb's, the safe lay securely nested in concrete. It required three and a half turns of the key to free its multiple bolts.

'You see? In this case.'

The door open, Pershore reached familiarly for a red morocco attaché case with a gilt monogram which lay on one of the steel shelves. But then, holding it in his hand, his expression changed to one of almost laughable bewilderment.

'It – it feels empty!'

'Haven't you got the key?'

'Yes, but it's too light . . . !'

In a sort of panic he dragged a key ring from his

pocket and fumbled at the locks. Inside, the case was lined with scarlet silk. But it contained nothing except the smell of expensive leather.

'This is fantastic – an outrage!'

The mayor-elect was bubbling with indignation and bafflement. Every cliché of injury came thronging to his lips.

'In the first place it's impossible – I shall get in touch with the chief constable! What are things coming to – what are the police being *paid* for!'

'Would you mind checking the contents?'

'I shall write to my M.P.!'

'At the moment it would help—'

'This is utterly criminal!'

Shrugging heavily, Gently turned his attention to the safe. Inside, everything seemed to be in scrupulous order. The door was immaculate in its dull green paint. Force had obviously not been used to effect an entry.

'You are sure that the money was placed in the safe?'

'Must you be so infernally stupid!'

'Have you had it open since the money was put in?'

'I have had no occasion to – the old fool sold over my head!'

'I would be very greatly obliged if you would check the contents.'

At last Pershore got down to it, still reverberating impotently. He was in such a way that he could scarcely remember what should be there. It was some time before he had established to his own satisfaction that, apart from the money, the contents were intact.

'Can you describe what you did after you drew the money?'

'Haven't I made it clear enough? I put it in the safe!'

'When you left the bank you drove directly back here?'

'Yes – I told you. And then I got that telephone call!'

It took time and patience to get information from Pershore. He was raving with the incredible wrong which had been done him. Bit by bit it had to be dragged out, with the chance of an insult at every fresh question.

'What time did you go to the bank?'

'How the devil should I know?'

'On Thursday morning you called in at the mill. Had you the money with you at that time?'

'I don't know – ask Fuller. He may have seen me with it!'

'It's important that you remember.'

'For heaven's sake, talk sense!'

'Who knew you had it or were going to draw it?'

'Do you think I'd broadcast a thing like that?'

'Where else did you go in Lynton that morning?'

'Nowhere, I tell you.'

'Did you have a drink at The Roebuck?'

'No, I did *not*!'

Slowly but remorselessly the picture was teased into detail. As he put his questions Gently wandered over to the study's two big windows. Here they were at the back of the house, facing a long stretch of terraced lawn closed by shrubberies. Immediately under the windows were flowerbeds shaped in scallops, but the naked earth, ideal for footprints, was rendered sodden and crumbled by the beating rain.

The windows themselves were wooden sash frames secured by common fingertip catches.

'When you went to draw the money, where did you park your car?'

'Honestly, Inspector! Outside the bank.'

'Were there many people about?'

'I really didn't notice.'

'That attaché case is conspicuous. Are you sure you caught nobody eyeing it?'

'Quite sure.'

'Who opened the door when you returned here?'

'Nobody opened it – I let myself in.'

'Then your servants knew nothing about it?'

'Not unless they saw me go out with the case.'

'Would that have been probable?'

'Do you really expect me to remember such things?'

'Where do you keep the safe key?'

'Attached to a body-belt, as you are aware.'

'Was the money ever out of your hands?'

'Never at any time until I deposited it in the safe.'

'And you can't remember whether you drew it before or after you visited the mill?'

'Not to swear to it, but it might have been after.'

'How long after you got back did the telephone ring?'

'Almost as soon as I got in the door.'

'You kept the case in your hand all the time you were answering it?'

'I put it on the desk there.'

'Nobody else was in the room?'

'Nobody.'

'You had your eyes on it?'

'All the time.'

'And then you put it in the safe?'

'Yes, just across the room!'

'Think: did you stop *anywhere* except at the mill?'

'I've told you already—'

'May I use your phone, please?'

Pershore watched him loweringly as he dialled the headquarters number. Like many an angry man before him, the mayor-elect had been sobered by the probe of Gently's interrogation. It was humiliating to be shown how little one really remembered about things . . .

'Gently here. Anything come in?'

Through the window came the steady beat of the rain on the lawn and flowerbeds outside.

'Never mind . . . get me Inspector Griffin, if he's there.'

He'd got the meat out of Prideaux Manor: it was up to the local boys to scoop up the gravy. Just at the moment, he could think of much more interesting things to be done.

CHAPTER TWELVE

For a second time that day Gently's Wolseley came to a halt among the puddles of the mill yard. If anything it was raining harder now, and the light was worse than ever.

The double doors of the engine-room were half-closed to keep out driving rain; a couple of men, making a dash from the sack-store to the passage, had sacks pulled over their heads and shoulders.

Was ever there such a day of rain before? When you pictured to yourself an English spring . . .

Gently, apparently, was in no hurry. Having parked the car he lit his pipe and remained in the driving seat puffing at it. First Fuller appeared at his door, ghost-like, his dark eyes almost black against his pale face; then the foreman peered out of the hoist-doors above the loading bay, pausing to spit into the yard below.

As for Blythely, he was no doubt having a nap. The bakehouse door stood ajar, but there was no sign of activity within. His wife Gently had seen in the shop.

She was reading a woman's magazine with a glossy cover. Come storm, come shine, the Blythely household continued to go about its routine . . .

Now there was a movement in the doorway of the sack-store. Blacker had come down and was rolling himself a cigarette. Looking anywhere but at the Wolseley, he licked the paper and dabbed it down; lighting up, he made an exaggerated face as though the match were scorching him.

Then he leaned against the doorpost, exhaling self-conscious lungfuls of smoke. His eyes seemed fixed on a point in the sky above the roof of the café across the road.

And still the rain poured out of the sky, and Gently continued to sit in the Wolseley.

Blacker grew restive. He shot a calculating glance at the engine-room, the next point of refuge, then, lowering his eyes, at the front wheels of the Wolseley. He dashed out his cigarette with a nervous movement. Twice he made as though to run for the engine-room doors.

But, finally, it was the Wolseley which attracted him. Like a magnet which he was forced to obey, it drew him away from the quick rush to the engine-room.

Frowning stupidly in the rain he thrust his head close to the driver's window:

'You want something, do you, coming here like this . . . ?'

Presumably Gently heard him, though he gave no sign of it. Behind the slightly misted window Blacker could see him smoking in comfortable dryness. Feeling the rain chilling his shoulders, the foreman rapped on the window.

'It's about that scooter, ain't it? I watched the bloke go in after me! I'm getting wet . . . !'

He was, and no mistake.

'Why don't you ask me, 'stead of keeping me standing here?'

Only the rain made him any sort of an answer.

Miserably, the foreman rapped again. Now that he was standing by the car it seemed impossible for him to retire without getting some acknowledgment of his action. His eye fell on the door-handle, but he wasn't bold enough to turn it.

'If it's about the money, that's what I earned, do you hear! I've been saving it up . . . Mr Fuller, he give me a bonus!'

Surely this should interest Gently, unless he was in some sort of a trance!

'It's my wages, that's what it was . . . I get sixteen pound a week! I've been keeping my eye on that scooter since the other side of Christmas. Why don't you ask me proper if you want to know? Look, I can't stop here any longer!'

Nevertheless, he seemed very reluctant to go, though by now his clothes were dragging from him like dishclouts.

'Haven't you heard what I've been saying . . . ?'

It was almost a whine, a plea to be noticed.

'It's the truth, I tell you, those fivers come in my pay

envelope! Why can't you say something, 'stead of just sitting there?'

A smoke-ring appeared perfectly around Gently's pipe. Blacker could see it circling as it drifted tenuously towards the roof. Cursing, he turned and ran slopping into the engine-room – the swine had wanted him to get wet, that was all that could explain it!

Shaking himself like a dog, he stood between the two doors and scowled at the rainbound Wolseley.

When at last Gently made a move it was for the side door of the miller's office, but having entered by it he seemed no more disposed to begin business than before.

First, he had got a little wet – that had to be seen to! He contrived to upset the whole office while putting his raincoat to dry on the backs of two chairs. Then he wanted a towel – hadn't anybody got one? And what about some hot coffee? Surely . . . with the café so close!

If there had been any work going on, it was disrupted by this time. Apart from anything else he had annexed the chairs – two for his raincoat and one for himself. And now that Mary had gone out, wrapped to the eyes, he was amusing himself by tapping out test sentences on her typewriter – surely a Yard man had better things to do with his time?

Fuller, without a dash of colour in his cheeks, got a file out of a cabinet and pretended to be looking through it. Having nowhere to sit he leant against his desk, but somehow he couldn't find a posture which was comfortable.

'We're getting some of these.'

Fuller started at the sound of Gently's voice.

'They're re-equipping some of the offices . . . a few of us got together. As a rule it's all done by contract, but we got permission to indent for this model.'

He had his back turned to the miller, and Gently's back was peculiarly unexpressive. As for his tone of voice, it contained nothing but an interest in Fuller's typewriter . . .

'Government departments are very conservative, you understand.'

He was tapping away afresh with two clumsy fingers.

'We've been using the same make since typewriters came in – a lot of taxpayers' money going all in one direction! For typing reports—'

Fuller threw down his file. 'If you've come here for something—!'

'Tabulation isn't a "must", but it's useful for paragraphing.'

'I've seen the lunchtime paper!'

'As a rule we like the larger typeface.'

The miller clenched his fists and groaned. Like his foreman, he was finding it far worse to be ignored than to be attended to by Gently. If you knew where you stood, that could be bad enough; but to be treated as though you were already in the bag . . . !

'It was one of them, wasn't it?'

The typewriter rattled.

'And this morning I was fool enough to tell you—'

In fact, that he'd been driving past the spot at midnight last night, alone.

The bell tinkled, and Gently pulled out his sheet. It may not have been a brilliant piece of typing, but such as it was it seemed to find favour with the man from the Central Office. He laid it across the typewriter and studied it fondly. From a back view, at least, he appeared to be completely absorbed.

'May I give you some advice?'

Offhandedly he threw out the question. Fuller, his lips tight in a bitter line, lifted his head to stare savagely at the bulky shoulders.

'Why not tell me the truth . . . now, without going any further? I know pretty well that you had nothing to do with either of the murders.'

The response was astonishing: Fuller began to weep. He collapsed against the desk and covered his face with his well-cared-for hands.

For two minutes by the pendulum clock he simply sobbed, foolishly, unconvincingly. And yet there was something terrible about this man behaving like a child.

'My wife—!' His broken voice sounded silly; he knew it and broke off, fighting to gain control.

'How can you understand—?'

That, too, seemed to have no meaning.

Gently had crumpled his sheet of typing and dropped it into the waste-paper basket. Mary, coming in streaming, was bundled promptly out again minus the thermos she had been clutching. As an added precaution Gently shot the bolts of both the side and the street doors.

'If I tell you . . . it's impossible! Nobody would believe—'

In a corner cupboard were the office cups and saucers. The coffee, steaming hot, had milk and sugar already added.

'Here . . . drink this!'

Gently shoved a cup into the miller's hand.

'I don't want any—'

'Drink it!'

The miller did as he was bid.

Like a fish in an aquarium, Mary was staring through the glass panels of the side door. But then the rain got the better of her curiosity and she disappeared in search of cover. They were isolated by the downpour. The little office seemed entirely cut off.

'How do you pay your men?'

'—my men?'

Fuller repeated the words vacantly.

'Yes. Do you cash a cheque, for instance?'

'Mary . . . she sees to it. She takes a cheque when she goes to lunch on Fridays.'

'She has a list, has she – so many fivers, ones, tens, etc.?'

'Not fivers of course, just ones, tens, and silver.'

'It was the same last week?'

'Except being Good Friday . . .'

'Has Blacker been after you for money?'

The miller shuddered. 'No . . . it was just being foreman.'

Gently nodded and sipped his coffee. Deadened by

the rain, the naphtha engine's beat sounded remote and subterranean. It had something of the quality of a barbaric drum-roll.

'You know that red morocco attaché case of Mr Pershore's?'

'I've seen him carry one.'

'Was he carrying it on Thursday?'

'Yes, he had it with him.'

'Was it in his hands all the while?'

'I didn't see him put it down.'

'What was Blacker doing at the time?'

'Him and Sid . . . they were feeding grain.'

'That night, which way did you come from the Spreadeagle?'

Fuller shuddered again and looked for somewhere to stand his coffee cup. His hands were trembling so much that it was a wonder he hadn't dropped it.

'You know then . . . ?'

'Isn't it obvious?'

'But if only you could understand!'

He was near tears again, huddled up there against his desk.

'To be frank, wasn't it amateurish? Two people got to know about it.'

'—two?'

'Blythely knew. He was watching the whole time.'

The blood rushed back into the miller's cheeks. He stared wildly at Gently as though challenging the truth of the assertion. Then he dropped his eyes to the floor, red to the tips of his ears.

'Oh, my God, what a mess!'

The words came in a hoarse whisper. Making no reply, Gently poured himself some more coffee from the thermos. In London, in Paris, who would have turned their head at such a business? But here, in Lynton . . . yes, it was a mess all right!

'Why haven't you arrested me?'

'It isn't breaking the law.'

'But being there at the time . . . the keys . . . everything . . .'

'It would have helped if you'd told me the truth in the first place.'

'You'd never have understood . . .'

That was his leit-motif. In fact, Gently had seen the pattern repeated a score of times. An attractive woman, a man bored and rebellious – add the opportunity, and what other answer was there? It was only the background . . .

'She . . . she wanted a baby.'

Awkwardly, Fuller was trying to tell him.

'They've never been able to – Blythely, too – he's got queer ideas! And Clara . . . you've only got to look at her. Can't you imagine what it must be like for her?'

A passionate woman tied to a stone-cold man.

'How did it happen?'

'God knows! It was always round the corner. Then one day when I was alone she came into the office with the rent for the bakehouse. Somehow, leaning over me . . . after I kissed her she cried, and I knew how badly . . .'

'How long has it gone on?'

'A couple of months – three, maybe.'

'And you always used the hayloft?'

'No! That was the first time we'd ever . . .'

The first time, and the poor fool had to get caught up in a homicide affair! In a grim sort of way, there was something humorous about it. Fuller had the makings of a man to whom bad luck came naturally.

'You'd best tell your wife. It'll probably have to come out.'

'My wife . . . it'll kill her!'

'Don't be so conceited! Wives sometimes surprise one.'

'You don't understand . . .'

They were back to it again.

A lorry came into the yard, backing and turning to get by Gently's awkwardly parked Wolseley. The driver came running to knock on the door, but Fuller made no attempt to unbolt and let him in.

'You think you can go against them . . .'

The lorry-driver, no doubt cursing, had given up his quest and retired.

'It seems easy, but even if nobody knows . . .'

'You have to live by the laws of the society that accepts you.'

Fuller looked up at him quickly, his dark eyes surprised. At that moment the naphtha engine coughed to a standstill, making a sudden silence in the twilit room. Just then there was only the sound of the rain.

'Now suppose you tell me what happened from the time you left the Spreadeagle?'

Boiled down it was less, very much less than Gently had hoped for. It seemed hardly possible that the miller could have been on the spot and seen so little. He had slipped away from the Spreadeagle in time to meet Mrs Blythely at half past eleven. The rendezvous had been at the stable door. On his way thither he had apparently noticed nothing, except that it was a cool evening and that road traffic had been light. He could remember no cars parked near the entry in Cosford Street.

'It was a clear night but no moon. You couldn't see a great deal once you got into the drying-ground. Clara was already there waiting for me, a coat over her nightdress. As you might suppose, we didn't waste a lot of time.'

'Are you absolutely certain you didn't see or hear somebody? Remember that Blythely wasn't far away, and presumably Blacker was in the offing.'

Fuller's head drooped wretchedly, but now he was almost eager in his desire to help.

'In the circumstances, one . . . after kissing her we went straight up. I'm pretty sure I didn't notice anything. Clara . . . she had a lot of time to make up!'

'What time did you leave?'

'We had an hour together.'

'And as you were coming away?'

'I'm sorry . . . all I was thinking about . . .'

One thing only was clear as daylight. Blacker had been in the yard and witnessed the rendezvous. In the morning he tackled Fuller in his office. He made no bones about what he was after.

'He'd seen us together – must have done some

eavesdropping. Anyway, he'd known beforehand and decided to watch. I wanted to knock him down, but God! what could I do? To give me time to think I made him foreman as he asked me.'

'He threatened to tell your wife?'

'Her, and Blythely.'

'Coming from a source like that . . .'

'It was true, and I couldn't have faced it out.'

'Again, you could have come to us.'

The miller made a despairing gesture.

'Anyway, I didn't have the time . . . and when I realized my position . . . !'

Gently nodded without pressing the point. There were limits in the pursuit of wisdom. He poured out the last of the coffee into their respective cups and tossed his off in several large mouthfuls.

'And now you know that Blythely knows?'

'It's – it's an impossible situation!'

'You can't just cut and run. You'll have to go and have it out with him.'

'But if you only knew the man! It's impossible to talk to him. He'll probably pretend he doesn't know what I mean, but all the time he'll use it as a lever . . . he just builds things up. I know how it will be.'

'Nevertheless, you've got to be neighbours.' Gently reached for his raincoat and began to put it on. 'And I'll let you into a secret. I've been giving him a lot of thought. He's the loneliest man in Lynton . . . just put that up your sleeve! If he doesn't want to forgive it's because he's desperate for a tie with someone.'

And he shoved out into the rain before the miller could ask him questions.

Outside he came to a halt, realizing that he wanted to use a phone. There was one in the office, of course, but after having made such a satisfactory exit . . . instead, he plodded across the road to the call box beside the café.

'Chief Inspector Gently – anything for me yet?'

He had lost count of the times he had put the same question since breakfast that morning.

'Yes, sir. We've found out the place.'

'What?'

'The place where Roscoe and Ames were staying. It was a pub at Strangemere, about eighteen miles away. But I'm afraid the chummy got out ahead of us, sir.'

Gently sighed softly and eased his shoulders into a good functional position with the glass panels of the call box. On the whole, he hadn't been expecting too much!

'Give me the details.'

They were few and unsensational. At Strangemere, apparently, a bird sanctuary attracted visitors, and occasional enthusiasts were found staying in the village. Roscoe had had the wit to take advantage of this circumstance. He had represented himself and Ames as London bird-lovers on vacation. Dressed in tweeds and equipped with binoculars, they had occasioned no attention; it was late in the day before the local bobby realized that he too had been fraternizing with a pair of rare birds . . .

'Arrived there on Friday, did they?'

'Yes, sir, driven in by a hire car.'

'Did they have any visitors?'

'No, sir, not as far as we know. But Roscoe had a letter yesterday with a Lynton postmark.'

'What happened last night?'

'Ames went off on the bus, sir. Roscoe said he might be late back and stayed up waiting for him. In the morning Roscoe packed his bags and went off in a hire car from the village. He left a message behind as though Ames would be coming back during the day, then later on the publican got a telegram asking him to forward Ames's luggage to an address in Stepney.'

Gently clicked his tongue. 'That was all very elaborate! And I suppose you discovered where the hire car took him?'

'To Ely station, sir.'

'Yes . . . that was inevitable. And then after that?'

'I'm sorry, sir, but Ely can't trace him.'

Gently sighed again. This was where he'd come in – with the solitary difference that now it was one man going the rounds! He riffled the edges of the phone book with a fretful finger. One left out of the three who knew all the answers . . .

'Listen – I want a search warrant for these two addresses. I'll be in to collect it as soon as it's signed.'

Outside a green Bentley had just stormed past into town – Pershore going to blow up the super, without doubt. Between the doors of the engine-room one could barely make out a face. As it felt Gently's eye on it, it shrank into the shadows.

CHAPTER THIRTEEN

THROUGH THE RAIN and early darkness the shop windows sparkled with a particular invitation and cheerfulness, though, when you looked through them, you discovered that the shops were nearly deserted. Some, in fact, had already begun to put up their shutters. It was only the larger shops and chain-store branches which were persisting in wearing out a fruitless day.

Blacker, seated beside Gently, had become silent and brooding. His earlier protests and asseverations had died away in occasional mutterings.

Of course Fuller had been lying! Wasn't Gently up to that? Those fivers had come via his wage packet and a bonus on his promotion . . .

'It's only his word against mine – don't know why you're making all the fuss! And he's got plenty to hide. If some of us saw fit to open our mouths . . .'

But Gently wasn't buying anything. He'd spoken only ten words to Blacker. Shepherding him through the rain to the Wolseley he'd said:

'You're coming with me. I'm going to search your house.'

After which he couldn't be teased into adding another syllable. So Blacker had stopped wasting his sweetness on the desert air.

The market square was a faintly gleaming vacuum, its shadows dappled by parsimonious street lighting. The green Bentley parked challengingly outside headquarters confirmed an earlier guess of Gently's.

'Superintendent Press engaged?'

The desk sergeant made a face and raised his eyes to the ceiling. Blessedly muted, one could hear the voice of the mayor-elect laying down the law on the floor above.

'I'll take my warrants . . . put me through to the St George.'

Dutt, looking drier, joined him at the car. Surprisingly enough, the rain was beginning to slacken. As they drove round the square it eased to an intensity which was almost commonplace.

'I give the desk a ring, sir.'

Dutt always liked to keep up with the latest developments.

'Other things being equal, sir, it looks like these geezers was on a burgling stunt. That Steinie bloke must have learned how to tickle peters.'

'Hmp!' Gently didn't sound very enthusiastic. 'And then he goes and banks his first split of stolen notes . . .'

'It could have been legit, sir. They might have cleaned up some mugs at Newmarket. Then they gets to hear of this Lynton nob with a safe-full of ackers – he was there at the time, sir. He might have shot his mouth to someone about what he was going to do.'

'Which transformed Taylor into a peterman?'

'Unless they figured how to get the key, sir.'

'And then they quarrelled amongst themselves?'

'I can't think of nothink else, sir.'

Gently drove on silently for some moments. In the back of the car, Blacker was listening avidly to their conversation. Gently could see him in the mirror leaning forward to catch every word.

'Let's hope Griffin is being his conscientious self . . . I shall be interested to hear details of his findings at Prideaux.'

Spooner Street, where Blacker lived, was part of the dismal nineteenth-century development of the north of the town. Cramped terraces of slate-roofed brick extended identically on either side. A handful of street lights, sparkling through the rain, seemed overawed by the implicit gloom of the thoroughfare.

'This is his, sir. Number one-one-four.'

It was no different from the others, about twelve feet of frontage. Beside it a party-passage led into the backyards. Many years ago all Spooner Street had been decorated in reddish-brown.

'Here's the warrant – take a look at it!'

Blacker scowled at it summarily.

'I can tell you right now you won't find nothing . . .'

'Just open the door, if you don't mind.'

Reluctantly the foreman brought a key out of his

pocket. As they entered the small front room they were met by the close, seedy smell of dry rot. Lit by a single clear-glass bulb of low wattage, the box-like compartment had an air of neglect and despair.

'Start in here, Dutt.'

'Yessir.'

'I'll take a look at the back.'

Blacker threw himself into a shoddy fireside chair, something like a grin twisting his weak mouth. Gently shoved open a door which led past stairs into the back parlour. From there one entered a scullery with access to the yard.

Switching on a torch, he played it round the shining walls and concrete outside the back door. As Dutt had informed him, there was no back way out of No. 114 – though, to be strict, if somebody had had the patience to scale a couple of dozen party-walls . . .

The floor of the yard was completely concreted and contained nothing but the dustbin and an old dog-kennel. From over the wall came the smell of kippers being grilled and the voice of a woman scolding children. The earth closet yielded nothing, neither did the coalshed, from the walls of which bunches of onions were hung.

'There's a loose board in here, sir!'

He went back into the front room. Dutt, that paragon of painstaking, had already rolled back the threadbare carpet. One of the planks underneath it was innocent of fastenings; it creaked invitingly when you put a foot on it.

'Go on – have it up!'

Blacker had lit a cigarette. His greyish eyes were watching them with contemptuous malice.

'If you ask me it was the gas people what had that board up, but nobody around here is going to ask me!'

They had it out. He was right. There was nothing under it except dirt and a gas pipe with a repair done to it. The foreman blew triumphant lungfuls of smoke towards the ceiling.

'Coming in here . . . doing what they like – never as much as "by your leave"! That's a fine way to treat an honest man, I must say! And isn't it us what pays their screw for them?'

'Get out of that chair.'

'What – are you going to have that to bits?'

Poker-faced, Gently removed the seat and prodded the upholstery. He was drawing a blank, he knew. Blacker's attitude was eloquent of what they were going to find there. Growing more insolent every moment, he followed them about with jeering remarks. He even went as far as to point out another loose board to Dutt.

'Now – do I get an apology?'

In a different way there was something almost like Pershore about him.

'You've pulled all my things around and you was wrong, wasn't you? So I reckon I ought to get an apology, don't you?'

Gently studied him mildly for perhaps ten seconds.

Involuntarily the foreman's eyes sank before this harmless-seeming scrutiny.

'Come on, Mr Blacker – we'd better be going.'

'Eh?' Blacker reared up. 'Where are we going to?'

'Where did you expect?' Gently shrugged indifferently. 'To the next obvious place. And your lady-friend may be out unless we get round there sharpish.'

With infinite slowness the rain was fretting itself to a standstill, becoming first a drizzle and then a fine mist. An uncanny silence seemed to follow in its wake, a silence belonging to the streets and buildings. It was as though they were emerging from a prudent retirement into which, animal-like, they had been driven by the hours of downpour. Now they were stirring and reaffirming their identities.

'She's nothing to do with me – how many more times—!'

Couldn't Gently afford that ironic little smile? Dutt was in the back keeping the panicky foreman company; his hand rested on the man's arm by way of an official reminder for him to watch his manners. And Blacker, he was sitting on needles; there wasn't any insolence about him now.

'I just go out with her sometimes – nothing wrong with that, is there? How should I know what she gets up to!'

People were beginning to come out in raincoats and plastic macs. A gang of youths were risking their fancy jackets and wrinkled trousers.

'She's a bad lot for all I know, but what's that got to do with me?'

In the cinemas they would be sitting in close-packed rows, adding the warm smell of damp clothes to the stale atmosphere of cigarette smoke.

'Anyway, I'm not to blame!'

They were turning down by Hotblack Buildings.

'What she does is her business – you can't pinch me for it!'

The Wolseley purred to a halt opposite the last wretched house.

Gently knocked his double knock and after an interval the door opened to reveal Maisie Bushell's aggressive features. She was wearing a purple dress with a short hemline and plunging neck, and her face was made up heavily with an abundance of eyeshadow.

'You! I can't see you now – I'm just off out!'

'I regret, Miss Bushell—'

'Take your big foot out of my door!'

'Please examine this warrant . . . we are here to search your house.'

'You get out of here, or I'll scream my bleeding head off!'

She didn't scream, she knew better, but nothing could quieten her virulent tongue. Gently, who had a wide experience of Metropolitan prostitutes, was surprised at the freshness and vigour of this sample of local talent . . .

'And you – bringing these so-and-so's into my house – me, what's never had no bloody trouble, except once when I asked a plain-clothes slop for a light!'

In spite of his anxiety Blacker was forced to wince under the flail.

'You're no stinking man – you're a so-and-so, do you hear me? I've had better men than you coming after me on their knees!'

'I didn't bring them here—'

'Like hell, you rotten juicer!'

'You listen, Maisie! I tell you—'

'Shut your filthy gob before I mess in it!'

Gently glanced around the miserable room with its apology for furnishings. He hadn't particularly noticed it before, but apart from one chair all the moveables were grouped on the same side. By the chair in question the furious owner had taken her stand.

'Would you mind stepping aside, Miss Bushell?'

'Yes, I bleeding would – so what are you going to do about it?'

'I shall have to remove you forcibly, ma'am.'

'Just you randy slops lay one finger on me—!'

It was Dutt who had to do it, at some personal risk and expenditure of energy. The voiced opinions of Miss Bushell would have coloured an air more susceptible. Raging and fighting, she was deposited on her settee; Dutt was obliged to stand by her while Gently prosecuted his search.

'You rotten buggers . . . leave that chair alone!'

The chair removed, it was possible to roll back the dingy floorcloth from the better part of the floor.

'If you touch my carpet I'll have your bloody eyes out!'

197

Nevertheless, the floorcloth was duly removed from the naked boards.

There was no need to go all the way. The half-plank, freshly sawn across, stood out like a bent penny. It was in almost the same situation as the loose board in Blacker's front room: the one had probably suggested the other.

'You touch it and I'll kill you!'

Unheeding, Gently prised up the plank and reached for the brown-paper packet which lay snugly underneath. He placed it on the chair and pulled the bow-knot which secured it; spilling out untidily came a number of made-up packages of what were indubitably five-pound notes . . .

'That's the so-and-so you want to talk to – me, I never knew nothing about it!'

Blacker's thin lips were bitten tight together, and at a glance from him towards the door, Dutt had moved across to plant his burly form in front of it. Gently was still counting the packages of fivers. There were nineteen of them, and one broken open.

'Asked me to keep it for him – do you think I bothered to look inside? As if a mess like him ever had any money!'

In each full packet there were a hundred notes, in the broken one only forty. Plain rubber bands had been substituted for the printed wrappers of the bank.

'Asked you to keep it – when was that?'

'Last Thursday night – and well you know it!'

'About what time?'

'Half past stinking midnight!'

'And you didn't enquire what the parcel contained, though keeping it involved sawing a plank out of your floor?'

She was a fighter to the last, the Mussolini-chinned Miss Bushell. Sitting bolt upright on the settee, she had the appearance of a boxer, game if outclassed; at the sound of the bell she would come out mixing it.

'Would you like to describe what took place?'

'Nothing took place – I told you everything last time!'

'You told me that you made a round of the pubs and that Blacker kept you company. Are you telling me now that he found this parcel on a seat?'

Miss Bushell swore lustily and with a degree of talent.

'So he left me after the pubs turned out – what's the messing difference? He'd got some business to see to, that's what he told me, and if he tries to tell you different then he's a rotten liar!'

'He told you the nature of the business?'

'No, he something didn't!'

'But he left you at about half past ten?'

'More like eleven, since it's a slop who wants to know.'

'What happened then?'

'What happened? I went home! Do you think I hang about the streets after I'm fixed up for the night?'

'And Blacker arrived here at half past twelve?'

'That's what I said, ain't it? Him and that messing parcel! "I got something here worth a bit, Maisie," he says. "You'd better hide it away for me, just in case they come looking for it." And me being weak and good-hearted—'

'Were you in the habit of hiding things for people?'

'Me? Why, I never done a wrong thing in my life!'

'But you made no objection – even though "they" might come looking for it?'

'I'd been on the juice, I tell you – I never give it a thought!'

'But the next day, when you were sober. Wouldn't you have thought about it then?'

'So help me God, I'd forgotten all about it. I mind my own business, not half a dozen other people's.'

'Yet you lied to me yesterday.'

'Because him there told me to!'

'And you didn't know what the parcel contained?'

'No more than a dead nit!'

'Isn't that your handbag lying on the mantelpiece?'

Miss Bushell screeched and sprang up from the settee, but Gently, whose movements were deceptive, had got there ahead of her. In a moment the handbag was decanted on to a table. Amongst the nick-nacks and loose change there fell out a slim bundle of fivers . . .

'That's some money what he give me!'

'Though he wasn't the messer to have any.'

'He did – I tell you – oh, you rotten lot of bleeders!'

Gently picked up the broken bundle and compared the two sets of notes. The serial letters were identical and the numbers just short of being consecutive.

'You – I'll have your wallet.'

Blacker, beginning to look ugly, changed his mind on

the approach of a very solid-looking Dutt. There were eleven fivers in his wallet and all of them matched with the bundle. Along with them was the stamped and signed receipt for a motor scooter.

'Do you want to say anything?'

Blacker caught Miss Bushell's eye.

'She's a filthy liar, *she* is – that's all you're getting out of me!'

'This is a serious business, you understand?'

Blacker's lips were clamped together again. The lines in his sallow cheeks had set in a desperate obstinacy.

'Right – then we'll get down to it! I'm arresting you two on a charge of being in unlawful possession of money, being the property of Geoffrey Pershore, Esq. You're coming down to headquarters where there'll be a formal charge, and I should warn you that anything you say may be taken down and used in evidence.

'And, by way of a further warning, this is a holding charge – there may be something a good deal graver just around the corner!'

Blacker stared at him in a sudden bewilderment, a curious expression developing in his unpleasant eyes.

'What was that bit . . . who did you say the money belonged to?'

'To Mr Pershore. Did you want to make a statement?'

For a fraction of a second the foreman hesitated, then he shook his head stupidly and resumed his recalcitrant expression. Dutt, watching Gently, was surprised at the suppressed excitement he could recognize in his senior's face.

'Very well – we'll have the cuffs on him ... I particularly don't want to lose Mr Blacker!'

'You're not putting those things on me!'

Miss Bushell let out a wail of dismay.

'I'll tell them you did me—!'

Gently made a placating gesture.

'I'm sure that a professional like you knows how to come quietly ...'

Miss Bushell said something which was wholly unprintable.

At headquarters the super had left word that he wanted a conference, but he himself had been hustled away by the outraged mayor-elect. Gently, who was hungry, was not displeased to find an absent super. His mind often worked best over a meal, and just then he had plenty of thoughts to turn over.

On the steps, however, he was caught by an incoming Griffin, and the local inspector's brow of thunder cleared very little as he caught sight of Gently.

'The super's on the way – he's looking for you.'

'I'm going to have a meal. I'll be back directly.'

'He's out for blood, I can tell you ... that confounded man! I suppose you didn't form any opinion about the job?'

Gently shrugged and felt for his pipe, putting it into his mouth unlit.

'First, I'd like to hear what you found there. I only had a glance round myself.'

Griffin groaned, propping himself up against the

porch. 'What in the deuce was there to find, except that the study had been burgled? The servants didn't know anything . . . the gardener . . . our print men are still poking around, but either chummy used gloves or the domestics are too blasted efficient. Gloves, I'd say, because there was nothing on the safe.

'Do you think this bloke with a yacht for sale could be a lead in?'

'What else did you find in the study?'

'Nothing – I told you! One of those tuppenny-halfpenny window catches had been forced and there were some scratches round the keyhole of the safe door.'

'Not much there for Records to get their teeth into.'

'I know . . . it's chronic. And wouldn't it just have to be Pershore! But what did you have to do with it, that's what I can't make out?'

'Didn't he tell you?'

'He was too busy slanging me.'

Gently smiled into the distant reaches of a by-now starlit sky.

'Ask your sergeant . . . I've briefed him on developments. I'm going to wrap myself round something full of calories.'

'But has it a bearing on the burglary?'

Griffin caught his arm.

'Later on we'll discuss the case more fully.'

CHAPTER FOURTEEN

T HE SUPER WAS walking up and down – an unusual thing for supers to do – and apparently, to judge by his ashtray, was in the process of chain-smoking.

His office looked smaller by night though it smelled exactly the same. Sitting on a chair at the corner of the desk, Inspector Griffin was examining his nails with a defensive intentness. The windows, partly open to the soft, after-rain air, wore their curtains in the same position as during the daytime.

'Come in, Gently – accept my congratulations!'

The super rounded his desk to shake Gently by the hand.

'You've done us a favour, I don't mind telling you. I dare say you wouldn't know, up there in the Central Office . . . but down here, one can't ignore the personal element.'

Even opposite the office windows there were couples making love, some of them casting a furtive upward glance from time to time. The balmy air had spring in it, an elusive fragrance impossible to define. Winter had been washed away by that single Homeric downpour.

'You can't understand how relieved I feel, though I realize that there are some loose ends to be tied up. Griffin, I feel sure . . . especially with the fellow in a cell. Naturally, we shall obtain a remand tomorrow.'

Cars swinging round the corner by the St George sent the shadows of lovers criss-crossing over the square. Lynton again . . . but a different Lynton; would the faint odour of daffodils come from one of the covered-up market stalls?

'There's just one thing I'm not quite clear about.'

For supper Gently had had a cod steak and a lot of imported new potatoes with butter.

'You left word that the recovery of the money was to remain secret for the moment, and that news of the arrest was to be withheld from the press.

'Of course, you probably have a very good reason, and after the great service you have done us we are eager to cooperate. But in view of our position – I won't be more explicit! – I should very much like to lift that phone and talk to Mr Pershore.'

Gently sighed softly to himself and turned a chair back to front. The taste of cognac and coffee still lingered gratefully on his palate . . . also, just behind it, the flavour of rhubarb tart and cream.

'You know what I'm here after.'

Wasn't the real question whether he was ready for his pipe or not?

'My business is Taylor's murder, not incidental

robberies. The recovery of Mr Pershore's money happened to lie in the scope of the investigation.'

'There's some connection, you mean?'

A frown appeared on the super's boyish brow.

'I realize, of course, that this Blacker is an employee at the mill, but that, taken on its own—'

'There's a little more to it.'

'It definitely ties in?'

'It's the nub of the whole affair.'

The super sat down, as though he realized it might be a longer job than he had taken it for. At the other end of the desk Griffin ceased to explore his nails and began to give his efficient attention. Gently, coming to a snap decision, produced his sandblast and tin of tobacco.

'I'll put you in the picture as briefly as possible.'

For some reason they both wanted to watch him rubbing the two slices of navy cut between his hands.

'There are two angles to it – we'll take Roscoe's first. Roscoe, because just at the moment he still happens to be alive.

'Roscoe went to Newmarket with Ames and Taylor. It was a two-day meeting, and they put up at a hotel. Somewhere, in the hotel, in the street, on the race-course, they came by a certain piece of information, and that piece of information brought them hotfoot to Lynton.

'Having got there, they put up at the best place in town, and almost immediately began spending money like hail. We know pretty well how much they'd got.

Judging from Taylor's bank book it was a flat five thousand pounds. But there had been no recorded robbery either here or at Newmarket, the money would appear to have been safe, and from evidence at the hotel they were expecting a further and larger supply. Something in the neighbourhood of ten thousand, perhaps!

'We come to Thursday night. They spent the evening as usual, in the hotel. At approximately eleven-thirty Taylor went out alone, apparently for what was expected to be a shortish absence. When he hadn't arrived back by one a.m. Roscoe and Ames, evidently anxious, questioned the night-porter. Then, after a conference, they went out looking for him, going in the direction of Fenway Road.

'They returned nearly an hour later. They seemed angry as well as anxious. After a further conference they tipped the night-porter a pound, and left instructions for him to ring them the moment Taylor showed up.

'Taylor, of course, didn't show up – he was lying strangled in the flour-hopper – and in the morning Roscoe and Ames were overheard discussing him in angry terms. Towards lunchtime Roscoe went out and fetched the midday paper. It carried the news of the finding of the body in the stop-press.

'They were too shaken by it to go in to lunch, and shortly afterwards they checked out of the hotel – taking steps, nevertheless, to prevent Taylor's absence from being immediately reported to the authorities. They took a train to Ely from where it would be difficult to trace them, and then doubled back to a safe base near the scene of the operation.

'Now, you will notice, they were in a position to bring irresistible pressure to bear. Taylor had been murdered, and they were aware of the identity of the murderer or murderers. They used this pressure. Roscoe received a letter which contained, without doubt, instructions as to the time and place for the pay-off. Ames, the muscle man, was sent to collect it, and a few hours later he was discovered floating down the river.

'That brings us up to date from the point of view of Roscoe. This morning, once more, he was obliged to start on his travels. The question beside him is: will he carry on? – and personally, I don't think he has much option.

'The police are after him and so is the murderer, but there is a pretty big carrot dangling in front of his nose. If he can collect that carrot and come off unscathed, then there's a chance for him to jump the country and give both of us the slip.

'My hunch is that he's doubled back again and is going to have one more try.'

Gently fished up his matches and relit his pipe. A lifetime of trying to do it had never yet convinced him that one couldn't smoke while one talked. Across the square came two constables, walking satisfyingly in step. They were deep in conversation and paid no attention to the courting couples.

'I still can't see—' The super cleared his throat. 'You're suggesting that somehow this money is connected, but the fact is that it was still in the bank at the time of the Newmarket meeting.'

'That's just what I was thinking, sir,' put in Griffin. 'Mr Pershore didn't know he would need it until Tuesday or Wednesday of last week.'

'But on Thursday several people could hazard a guess.'

Gently blew a casual smoke-ring.

'Also, there was the preliminary five thousand – that was the initial gambit. Wherever it came from, it was safe and not likely to be missed.'

The super brooded over it with an expression of distaste. With the best will in the world, he felt on the defensive against Gently. Something was going to be pinned on to Lynton, he could feel it in his bones, but unless he was being denser than usual he failed to see how it was to be done.

'In effect you are saying that these three men . . . on the first occasion they cleared up all the ready cash. Then, redoubling their demands, they forced their victim to a desperate act – and this person was aware that Mr Pershore had made a large cash withdrawal?'

'Mmn.' Gently nodded. 'It could be something like that.'

'But this Blacker scarcely fills the bill – he wouldn't have had five thousand by him. And then again . . . well, he doesn't, does he? How could this Roscoe lot ever have heard about him at Newmarket?'

'Looks more like Fuller.' Griffin was following shrewdly.

'*He* might have produced five thousand at a pinch, *and* he would have seen Mr Pershore with his attaché case.'

'He did. I asked him.'

Gently shrugged indulgently.

'Also, he happened to attend that meeting at New-market.'

'Then surely, if there's a tie-up—'

'Let's get back to the facts first. Up till now, we've only been considering them from Roscoe's viewpoint.'

Both the super and Griffin looked as though they might have smart rejoinders up their sleeves, but neither of them hazarded one. Gently struck another match and tossed it into the super's ashtray. Downstairs at the desk they could vaguely hear the duty sergeant asking somebody questions.

'At the mill you'd got something going on which is happening every hour of the day and night – out there at the moment, as a matter of fact!

'Fuller had fallen for the baker's wife. They were neither of them people with much experience in conducting clandestine love affairs. At first it was just a kiss and cuddle in the office – the clerk having been sent out on an errand, no doubt. Then I dare say they laid plans for something more interesting, but they were stuck for an appropriate opportunity.

'It came on the eve of Good Friday when two events coincided. One of them was Fuller's stag party at The Spreadeagle, and the other the circumstance that the baker would be spending all night in the bakehouse.

How long ahead they had been making arrangements I didn't elicit, but what is certain is that they were very careless over them.

'Blythely, the baker, had got wind of the assignation, and Blacker knew even the time and place. As a result, when they met outside the stable in the drying-ground, two people were stationed there to witness the fact.

'Where Blacker was is conjectural, but he was certainly there. In the morning he used his knowledge to blackmail Fuller into making him foreman. Blythely, on the other hand, hid in a lean-to urinal. From there he could watch the stable but could see nothing of the yard.

'And the times of these dispositions were roughly from half past eleven till half past midnight: at that critical time there were four people on the spot.

'Fuller can tell us nothing, which is not surprising; nor, I imagine, can Mrs Blythely. They were in the hayloft busy with their own doings. Blythely, most unfortunately, could hear but not see, so we are left with Blacker as the solitary eyewitness.

'What Blythely did hear, however, is very suggestive. He heard three or four separate sets of footsteps. Giving approximate times he heard the first set at eleven-forty. They entered the yard from the opening into Cosford Road, came down the yard and halted in the passage between the mill buildings and the bakehouse block. Five minutes later a second set followed them. Blythely says they were lighter and quicker, like a child's, which suggests that they belonged to Taylor.

'There was a short conversation between these two people which Blythely was unable to overhear, neither did he hear them leave the passage. A third set came down the yard at about ten minutes to twelve. They lingered in the passage and then came back running.

'Finally there were steps from the passage at about twelve o'clock midnight – a little slow and hesitant, according to Blythely. Shortly after they had gone he may have heard a car started, but there was nothing further to report until the guilty party re-emerged at half past twelve.

'Out of that timetable, I expect, you can begin to reconstruct the murder.'

It was not the implications but the completeness of the information which was making Griffin turn hot. You could see what he was thinking, with his neck growing scarlet. They'd both had their turn at it, he and Gently – about the same time each, but what a difference in their results! Surely there was an element of luck in the affair . . . ?

'You seem to have covered a lot of ground.'

The super, too, was sounding stiff, but in his case it may have been the guilty pair who rankled.

'I suppose you're sure of your facts – testimonies reliable and all that? In a case of this sort I should scarcely have expected . . .'

'The evidence seems to dovetail fairly neatly.'

'Oh, I'm not suggesting we can teach you any-thing!'

'There's always a possible margin for error.'

The super ground out a cigarette butt, himself getting heated. More than ever he had the feeling that Gently was building up something unpleasant and reprehensible. To hide his chagrin, Griffin was also fiddling with a cigarette. Over it he muttered:

'As a matter of fact, I did suggest . . .'

Gently seemed lost in the dark world beyond the window.

'If you don't mind me saying so, it still isn't clear—'

'How the money ties in?'

'Exactly! Up till now—'

'Up till now the money has been a hypothesis – except that it was in Blacker's possession by about half past twelve on the Friday morning.'

'I agree that it's a coincidence.'

'Let me reconstruct what I think occurred.'

The super drew a deep breath and cradled his chin in his hands. On the square a mobile fish-and-chip saloon had drawn up, lending a scent of frying to the vernal atmosphere.

'We'll take it from Blacker's angle – I think that's most convenient. At some time between eleven and half past he secreted himself in the drying-ground.

'He saw first Mrs Blythely arrive and wait outside the stable. Then Fuller joined her, and when they had gone into the stable, Blythely came out of the passage to take up his position in the lean-to. Ten minutes later X came into the yard.

'X I am assuming to be the murderer. I don't know whether Blacker recognized him – there wasn't a lot of

213

light. But he saw him go down the yard and stop in the mill passage, and it's possible that he noticed the package X was carrying under his arm.

'At eleven forty-five X was joined by Taylor. After a brief conversation X handed Taylor the package, and as Taylor was examining it to make sure of the contents, X slipped behind him and effected strangulation.

'His plans were obviously made and he wasted no time about them. Immediately life was extinct he set about disposing of the body. How much of this Blacker witnessed is open to conjecture, but I think there is little doubt that it was he who Blythely heard come down to the passage a little later.

'There he stumbled over the package – partly open, one supposes – and discovering what it contained, made off with it at a run. X, having shot the body into the hopper, returned to pick up the money: its absence must have been a shock to him, but there was nothing he could do about it and he didn't hang around.

'Unless I've overlooked something, that seems to me the inevitable interpretation.'

'I don't agree at all!'

Griffin was ready to jump in directly.

'Surely there's another alternative that fits just as well?'

'There may be.' Gently bowed his head. 'It's difficult to think of all the variations . . .'

'Suppose it was Taylor in fact who committed the robbery – suppose he'd had to hide the money in the mill, for some reason. Then Blacker catches him collecting it – there's a struggle, and Taylor is strangled – isn't the hopper the very place where Blacker would get rid of the body?'

Gently shrugged without replying. Had he still to make himself plain? For most of the day he'd known the inexorable answer to all the questions . . .

'At least it simplifies it, Gently.'

The super wanted to buy Griffin's notion.

'It gets rid of that "X" of yours, who's likely to be a pitfall. And it gives us a clearer picture – the whole thing becomes more credible. This Roscoe lot had begun to dabble in burglary, and at Newmarket they heard of a likely crib to be cracked . . .'

Could neither of them see the facts which were staring them in the face?

'There are four people, I think, who know the murderer's identity.'

He would have to tell them in so many words.

'Roscoe knows, and I'm sure Blacker does. Then there's me, and of course, Mr Pershore.'

'What!'

The super sat up with a jerking movement.

'Mr Pershore . . . doesn't that follow? The money was his and nobody else's.'

'What's that got to do with it?'

'Why, everything, I imagine! It was he whom Roscoe and the others were blackmailing.'

The super leaned back with an expression of dizziness. A crazy element seemed to have crept into the exchanges! On the one hand, Gently didn't seem to be raving, but on the other . . . could he have heard him properly?

'But that money was stolen!'

Gently shook his head slowly.

'Ask Inspector Griffin what he found in the study at Prideaux.'

'He – he found it had been broken into. Didn't you, Griffin?'

'That's right!' fired Griffin. 'There's no question about that. A window catch was forced and there were scratch-marks on the safe.'

'Only' – Gently paused to make sure they were following him – 'there were no scratches or forced windows when I was there an hour earlier. They appeared between the time I left and the time when Inspector Griffin arrived.'

'Then you are saying—'

The super looked sick. Out of seemingly nowhere, his nightmare premonition was developing.

'I'm saying that Roscoe, Ames and Taylor came to Lynton to blackmail Pershore, and that he, very determinedly, has responded by killing two of them.'

Coffee was brought in by a woman from the canteen. It was none too warm and probably concocted from a powder. In the square the fish-and-chip saloon was doing excellent business; quite a group were clustering round it, eating from newspapers and greaseproof bags.

'Don't you see the improbability of it?'

At last there was a spell for Gently's pipe. Having got rid of his coffee, he scraped out the bowl and refilled it. After food, it was usually the second pipe which tasted the best.

'He's been a figure here for twenty years. After all that time, and with never the slightest suspicion . . .'

Round and round the super was gnawing at it, trying his best to find a weak place. Against anyone else, yes, it was a case – but against Geoffrey Wallace Pershore, Esq. . . . .

'We probably shan't know until we get hold of Roscoe.'

'Just ask yourself! What could they have dug up about him?'

'It might be something from a long time ago – before he ever set foot in Lynton.'

'He came from overseas.'

Griffin was childishly bent on getting his foot in somewhere.

'It was South Africa, I believe. I can remember it quite plainly. It was while you were still at Cheapham, sir.'

'South Africa, eh . . . ?'

'He was as brown as a berry – younger, of course, not much over thirty. There was a lot of gossip. He had a Bentley in those days. According to what they said, he'd made his pile out of palm oil or something.

'Anyway, he took a liking to Lynton and started investing his money here. Then, just before the war, he bought Prideaux Manor from old Major Calthorpe.

During the war he organized the local St John's Ambulance, and turned Prideaux Manor into a nursing-home.

'Everyone thought he'd get an Honours List mention.'

'Should've done!' wailed the super. 'It was only damned favouritism . . .'

'Since then he's done a great deal for Lynton. His name has been at the head of every charity list. He came to the assistance of the football club when it looked like going broke, and started the Library Appeal Fund with a thousand guineas.

'His brokerage business qualifies him for the council. He's been an alderman six years and was sheriff two years ago. Now, as I expect you know, he is to be the next mayor.'

'Quite a busy career, in fact!'

'Whatever you think of him, he's public-spirited.'

'And after twenty years he wouldn't want the good work blemished . . . especially by a trio of Stepney spivs.'

'But can you be *certain*, Gently!' the super moaned. 'It's such a fantastic idea – and if you happened to be wrong . . . !'

'I'll check off the points for you.'

Gently extended his clumsy fingers.

'All in all, I think you'll find they add up to a case.

'First, Pershore attended the meeting at Newmarket. Second, he was the source of the money. Third, he inspected the mill on the Thursday morning and knew about the flour-hopper. Fourth, he would have a set of keys to the mill. Fifth, he has no checkable alibi for the Thursday night. Sixth, his story about the money being stolen is unsupported by fact. Seventh, he manufactured evidence in an attempt to support it.

'Tomorrow, I hope, the bank will be able to tell us that he withdrew the first five thousand pounds a few days after the Newmarket meeting. As far as we're concerned, that will just about clinch it.'

'But it's all circumstantial – a defence would make hay of it.'

Gently hunched a shoulder. 'There's Roscoe to come! Also we've got an eyewitness tucked away in the cellar. I think Blacker will talk if you put it to him nicely.'

The super got to his feet and began pacing the room again. His distress was genuine and Gently felt sorry for him. Griffin, toying with his coffee-spoon, seemed caught between two contrary currents. He wanted to be loyal to the super, but nevertheless, as a policeman . . .

'Get Blacker up here!'

The super had made his decision.

'One way or another we've got to settle this matter.'

He glanced defiantly at Gently, but Gently was busy going through his pockets. Surely, in some neglected corner, there ought to be a peppermint cream?

CHAPTER FIFTEEN

L ATER ON, THE super had resigned himself to the calamity which had fallen jointly on himself and Lynton. After Blacker went he sat a long time brooding darkly over his two-tone desk.

Not that Blacker, though he had talked, had proved entirely satisfactory. His evidence was of the type which a defence counsel such as Pershore could brief would tear into fine shreds.

'There was a car standing in Cosford Road which looked like a Bentley . . . no, it wasn't stood under a light, nor I couldn't see the colour . . .

'Of course I saw him go down the yard . . . looked familiar, I thought . . . the little bloke, too . . . I didn't hear any struggle.

'Then I tumbled to it, when I heard whose the money was. That was Pershore all right, and I don't mind swearing to it.

'If I put it to them straight, are you going to get me off the other . . . ?'

Blacker had done some brooding of his own, sitting three hours in a cell with the smell of new cement in his nostrils.

But it was testimony that convinced the super, however vulnerable it might be to forensic corrosives. Gently's reconstruction was being corroborated every time the foreman opened his mouth. And behind it all loomed Roscoe, the man no counsel could shrug aside.

'Are you suggesting we make the arrest?'

He was trying to keep the bitterness out of his tone. The fish-and-chip saloon had departed for pastures new, and a clean, bright spring moon was climbing over the Georgian roofs and chimneys. Once or twice, from high overhead, they had distinctly heard the piping calls of migrant birds coming in from the sea.

'No . . . not yet. The case isn't foolproof.'

'You want to dig up his past?'

'Most of all I want Roscoe.'

'Aren't we doing all we can about him?'

'We'll have to take a risk.'

The super flashed a look at Gently, not quite understanding him. The man from the Central Office wore a stubborn expression which Dutt could have interpreted. His pipe, unlighted, stuck out of his mouth at an angle.

'Tomorrow I'd like Blacker remanded on that charge, but I don't want the money referred to. Have a word with the magistrate – it shouldn't be difficult. Substitute "stolen property" or something like that.

'And naturally, you'll fob off the coroner about Ames.'

'The press will be awkward.'

'Try and clamp down on them! They'll usually cooperate if it's in a good cause. Then I'd like Inspector Griffin to keep investigating that robbery – any sort of play-acting to keep Pershore happy.

'If he can get his prints we'll send them up to Records, and perhaps you've got a man who can do some quiet digging. That Upcher deal will bear looking into – it should hardly fit Pershore's story as neatly as he pretends it does.'

'And meanwhile, you think that Roscoe . . . ?'

'He'll get in touch with Pershore somehow.'

'We could check his mail and tap the phone.'

Gently shook his head.

'Look at it from Roscoe's angle – and he was the brains of the bunch. If he talks he's admitting blackmail. If he doesn't we have to prove it. And besides admitting blackmail, he'll be kissing goodbye to a gold mine.

'Unless we can catch the pair of them red-handed, we shan't have the benefit of Roscoe's evidence.'

'But Pershore will try to kill Roscoe!'

'That's our trump card – and we've got to play it.'

The super looked grave.

'It's a terrible risk, Gently . . .'

'Of course, I shall be prepared to take full responsibility.'

He got to his feet, the cold pipe still lolling from the corner of his mouth. How could he tell them that he

222

could see the whole pattern of it, as surely as though even now it was written up in a report?

'You don't have to worry . . . just keep Pershore from being suspicious. You'll find it'll work out. It isn't the first time . . .'

'If he succeeds in killing Roscoe—'

'We could probably establish method! Now, if you don't mind, I'd like to be turning in.'

The super did mind, but he could think of nothing to advance against it. He watched Gently go in helpless silence. When the door closed behind the bulky back his eyes met those of Griffin's. Suddenly, as though both men were thinking the same thought, each of them shrugged his shoulders.

The car Gently had was the super's Humber, and it was warranted to do better than a hundred m.p.h. Since Prideaux Manor lay at the end of a cul-de-sac, it was a simple matter to cover it by concealing the Humber in a side-turn at a safe distance.

Twice, during the morning, he and Dutt had seen Griffin go by in a police Wolseley. Agreeable to instructions, the Lynton inspector was doing his best to make a show of proceeding with his investigation. As he returned from his second journey he slowed and pulled into the side-turning.

'It could be this afternoon – he says he's got some business to see to.'

'Business that would take him out?'

'He didn't say, and I thought I'd better not ask him.

This morning at a quarter past eleven he had a telephone conversation, but he ordered me out of the study, so I don't know who it was with.'

'You're doing a good job.'

Griffin coloured and let in his clutch.

It was an almost perfect day following the miserable one which preceded it. Gently had been prevailed on to remove his jacket, and sat smoking in his shirtsleeves with the door of the Humber ajar. The sky, at first washed clear, was now chequered with small, fleecy clouds. In the plantation which flanked the lane a blackbird was singing; larks rose continuously from the field of young wheat beyond the hedge opposite.

'What a day for a blinking picnic!'

Dutt, like all cockneys, had a note of mute poetry in his soul.

'If I had the missus here . . . can't you see the nippers rousing around in them trees?'

From the radio they had had a bulletin from headquarters which told them little enough. Upcher, the yacht-owner, had been contacted and given an account of his deal. The price demanded for his craft had been twelve thousand five hundred and not ten, as Pershore had claimed, but the difference could easily be explained as a hoped-for compromise for immediate cash.

Of Pershore's past there was nothing to relate. After twenty meritorious years at Lynton the trail had vanished into unsubstantial rumour. Griffin had got his prints, and that might lead to something, but failing this it rested solely with Roscoe – a Roscoe picked up alive and communicative.

'Do you reckon it will be this afternoon, sir?'

Gently knew it would, with the irrational conviction that at times came to him. In every case there was a point when his vision seemed to border on the uncanny. Some people called him lucky, but in fact it went further than that.

'We might as well have our lunch.'

The St George had put them up a wicker basket of provisions. Undone, it displayed a truly old-fashioned lavishness: there was cold chicken and salad, apple turnover, biscuits, cheese, fruit, and four thermoses of hot coffee.

'Between you and me, sir, I reckon this Roscoe won't be such a mug as the other two charlies.'

'No . . . but he's up against a dangerous man.'

'He could lay for him, sir, and maybe put a bullet in him.'

'Not Roscoe, Dutt. He's a professional through and through.'

'All the same, he's in a rum position.'

They ate in silence, the countryside about them seeming to drowse in its peacefulness. Nothing passed along their lane or the road leading to the Manor. An early sulphur-yellow butterfly, unsteady in the brilliant sun, was the only moving thing to come their way.

Gently glanced at his watch, which showed twenty minutes to two. If lunch at the Manor was at one, it shouldn't be long before Pershore and the green Bentley . . .

He finished his coffee and screwed up the thermos. Just to test his intuition he would have the engine running! Dutt, taking the hint, packed the plates away in the basket. It was as though they had suddenly received a message that the quarry was on his way.

'If he sees us do you think we can hold him, sir?'

Gently pulled the door shut with a grunted reply. If Griffin had played his part properly Pershore should have no suspicion; if he had, well, there were the patrol cars to reckon with!

It was ten minutes to two when the Bentley swept past the lane-end. Pershore, sitting relaxedly at the wheel, had no eyes for the Humber lying half hidden behind the bend. Gently gave him plenty of rope. The Bentley was not being driven fast. The road from Prideaux to West Lyng, where it joined the main Norchester road, was fairly open and passed few side-turnings.

'Of course it might be like he says, sir, just a business trip or something.'

It might, of course . . . the chances were even.

'He don't seem in no hurry – hardly doing forty.'

Was Dutt deliberately setting out to be annoying?

At West Lyng Gently almost held his breath, waiting for Pershore to choose his direction. If it were left, the man was simply going into Lynton; he had, after all, plenty of business to see to there.

But Pershore turned right, swinging his big car round leisurely through a gap in the traffic. Wherever he was heading it was not for Lynton. Gently, breathing again, pressed harder on the accelerator. On the busy main road he needed to be closer to his game.

Shimmering under the spring sun, the dark surface extended ribbon-like across the rough heathland of West Northshire. For some miles there were no hedges, and the string of traffic ahead was firmly in view. Pershore made no effort to increase his pace. He seemed quite content to hold his niche between a Zephyr and a red-and-black Velox. If he had any idea that he was being followed, he was giving not the smallest indication of it.

'Got any idea where his nibs is off to, sir?'

Dutt, as usual, was beginning to puzzle away at it.

'I doubt whether it's Norchester.'

'More like the country, sir?'

'It could be anywhere, and that's the truth!'

Dutt pulled out a road map and began to frown over it. In his imagination Gently was already exploring the road ahead. Apart from odd villages the next place was Swardham, then East Cheapham, which was larger, and so to the city. All of them were equally likely or unlikely – you could get to any of them by rail from Ely.

Swardham was coming up now, a straggling, charming country town with a great flint-and-freestone church tower. The main road turned left across the top of a triangular plain, and then twisted downwards past a T-junction with traffic lights.

'Gawd, we're going to lose him!'

Gently sensed the danger and trod on the accelerator. The traffic lights blinked red but the road was clear, and the Humber soared through like an angry tiger. On the far side there was an S-bend ending in a murderous corner, and Gently, tempting providence, passed three vehicles while negotiating it. Then the road stretched away clear again up a long incline; once more they had the traffic ahead under surveillance.

'He's blinking gone and lost us, sir!'

It was woefully apparent. There was nothing now lying between the red-and-black car and the Zephyr.

'He may have opened her out . . .'

Gently kept the Humber sailing, but at the top of the rise, from which a long stretch was visible, there was still no sign of the majestic green Bentley.

Viciously Gently braked and reversed into a field-gate.

'Get on to headquarters – tell them to put a net round Swardham!'

'He didn't turn into the town, sir . . .'

'I know – which leaves two directions. Either he went south by that by-road we've passed or north at the T-junction – we take our pick!'

'After the lights I never saw him again.'

'We'll take a chance and try the T-junction.'

Again he had to shoot the lights, this time creating no little chaos. A constable came running and waving his hands, but subsided into a breathless salute as he recognized the car.

The junction road led to Fosterham and contained very light traffic. Gently set his foot down and saw the speedometer needle straying over ninety. On either side flashed by stony fields reclaimed from heathy breckland; a plantation in the distance loomed a long time against the sky.

Then they came to a fork, right beside the plantation. The Fosterham road continued to the right, to the left a minor road extended to Castle Ashton.

'Here – you over the hedge!'

The luck of good detectives was with him. A farm-worker had halted his team and drill to take a swig from a bottle of cold tea.

'Have you seen a green Bentley go past this way?'

'A big ole car—?'

'Yes, that'd be it.'

'Come by a coupla minutes ago – slowed to look at the signpost.'

'Which way did it go?'

'W' up there to Ash'n Castle.'

The Humber ripped away in a flurry of gear-changes. Ahead the inevitable square church-tower rose proudly from a long, high ridge of land. On the left, surprising and spectral, stood a group of remains of some ecclesiastical building; opposite to them, appended to the ridge, brooded massive and bosky earthworks. Between the two lay the village, lifting embattled up the slope.

They crossed a stream which might have served as a moat and swung up through the houses of mellowed local brick. At the top was a flint gateway and beyond it the village green. Parked there, but empty, stood Pershore's handsome car.

'Where can I find the owner of this car?'

Here there were several informants, two of them women stood gossiping with their prams.

'Didn't he go up that way . . . towards the castle?'

'That's right, mister. That's where you'll find him.'

From the green a narrow lane led between a brick chapel and the wall of a private garden. Twisting over a bank, it plunged suddenly into the tree- and bush-choked castle ditch, some seventy feet deep, and could be seen fretting its way up the huge mound on the other side.

'Quiet now – listen!'

Pershore couldn't be very far ahead. At the most, he would just have had time to climb the earthwork, and might now be amongst the bushes and fragments of masonry which crowned it. Distantly, from further round the mound, came the bleating of tethered goats.

'Follow me now – but keep it quiet!'

He went down the path half-walking, half-sliding. At the bottom it was curiously silent and airless, as though they had got to the bottom of a well. Going up the mound it was impossible not to make some noise. In places it was almost perpendicular, and one had to pull oneself along by the bushes and scrub.

Then, at the top, they were faced by the remains of a flint-rubble wall, with a fissure running through it just wide enough to scrape past. His head poking round it, Gently froze to a standstill. Either they were too early . . . or else they were too late!

From his vantage point he commanded the whole interior of the mound, a hollow amphitheatre sunk some thirty feet below the perimeter. To the south it fell away in a steep, bush-filled ravine, being protected at a lower level by outworks and the river. The wall which topped the perimeter was in places still substantial, and inside it ran a rough path a few feet in width. It was on this path that Pershore was standing only a short distance from the fissure; near him, but not too near, stood the elusive James Roscoe . . . a German Army-pattern Mauser sitting snugly in his hand.

'You don't have to look surprised, cock!'

Roscoe was a big man in his forties with a swarthy complexion and greasy dark-brown hair. He was wearing a green mixture Harris-tweed suit the jacket of which seemed tight across his shoulders.

'Cor luvvus – what did you expect, after knocking off Punchy and Steinie? This is the way I trust you, matey, wiv the safety catch off and one up the spout! And if I let me finger slip it's only taking bread from the hangman.'

He'd got the whip hand and he knew it, but he wasn't going to let the knowledge betray him into an indiscretion.

'Steinie, he was easy, wasn't he? Never even took a razor wiv him, poor little bastard! Then there was Punchy, big but stupid – he could handle you, Punchy could!

'But now it's me, who's big but not stupid, and what's more, I've brought a little clincher wiv me. So this time it's a deal, and you can thank your lucky stars – because if the bogeys ever gets me, matey, your number is up just as sure as Mick the Miller.

231

'You're not going to sit here stewing in lolly while Jimmy Roscoe rots in Wandsworth!'

'There's no need to be offensive, my man.'

It was almost a shock to hear Pershore being so coolly himself in such a situation. His back was turned to Gently, but his attitude was unmistakable; it was that of a leading citizen forced into distasteful conversation.

'You're no cleverer than your friends, as I think you're going to find. And just be good enough to remember who it is you're talking to.'

'Who I'm flipping talking to!'

Roscoe sounded as though he couldn't believe his ears.

'That's what I said. You're talking to the next Mayor of Lynton. However smart you think you're being, you'll kindly bear that in mind.'

Was it shrewdness on Pershore's part or couldn't he really help it? Roscoe, his eyes narrowing, obviously thought the latter.

'Oh, no you don't, old cock!'

The Mauser prodded forward.

'It'll take a better man than you—'

'Say "sir" when you speak to me.'

'For your own good I'm telling you—'

'I *will* have a proper respect!'

It was either madness or a naïve form of cunning. Roscoe now was wavering, uncertain which to believe.

'Cut it out, will you – let's get down to business!'

'First, my man, you will acknowledge who you're doing it with.'

'Get this straight, cocker, you're not getting Jimmy Roscoe's rag out. That flipping horse ain't going to run here—'

'Unless you cease to be offensive I shan't hand you a penny.'

For all his sharpness, Roscoe was baffled. This was outside anything he had prepared himself to expect. As a tactical manoeuvre he could readily understand it, but the trouble was that Pershore had the veritable ring of conviction . . .

'All right, then, old guv'nor, if that's how you wants it—'

' "Sir", if you don't mind.'

'Flipping "sir", then!'

'And please don't forget.'

Pershore visibly unbent a little. In his mind's eye, Gently could see the complacency stealing over the mayor-elect's heavy features.

Wasn't it a blend of both, that pose . . . a mixture of childishness and cunning? Wasn't puerility, perhaps, the key to the man's strange make-up?

He had stayed a child . . .

'Just because we have a transaction to make there is no need for you to presume upon it. This is simply a form of business like other forms of business. Our stations remain exactly the same as before.'

Their stations remained—! No wonder Roscoe was beginning to grin. The geezer was a screw loose, that's what he was thinking. He'd croaked Steinie and then Punchy – was that the behaviour of a charlie with all his marbles? – and now, stowed in a corner, he was beginning to show his trouble.

Broadmoor was where he was heading . . . if he escaped the eight o'clock walk!

'I think your price was fifty thousand pounds?'

Roscoe gulped. He had to play his part!

'That's right, old guvnor – *sir*, I mean to say! And I hopes you've got it safe and sound in that suitcase there.'

'You will realize that I had some difficulty in obtaining that amount of money. Fortunately I am a stockbroker myself and was able to raise it without attracting attention. In twenty-pound notes . . .'

'Here! I told you in fivers!'

'They would have been too bulky, Mr Roscoe.'

'You give me that suitcase!'

'A twenty-pound note is, I assure you, perfectly current.'

Sedately, Pershore laid the suitcase on the path and stepped back to enable the other to examine it. Roscoe, still with the Mauser trained, dropped to a crouch and snapped the catches with his left hand. Something like sweat was glistening on Gently's forehead . . .

'But this here ain't—!'

Roscoe got no further. Pershore was on him like a cat. With a nodule of flint he had held concealed in his hand, he was smashing incessantly at the bookmaker's head. The gun crashed harmlessly and rolled smoking down the slope. Roscoe, dazed by a blow which had found him, was trying to cover up from the murderous attack.

'This is how it's done, my man!'

There was something frightening about Pershore's terrible assurance.

'It's no use having a gun – this is the way I do them!'

In another moment he would have got the blow that counted past the bookmaker's drooping defence.

'Take him, Dutt!'

Gently hurled himself through the fissure. Dutt, following behind, rushed up to throw a strangling arm round the neck of the man his senior was grappling with. It was over almost as soon as it had begun. Pershore, choking and gasping, lay struggling with the handcuffs which had suddenly been clamped on his wrists. Roscoe, blood streaming from his head, was clutching at it and trying to stagger to his feet.

'Who is this man?'

Mercilessly Gently stood over him.

'He's a bloody murderer—!'

'But what's his proper name?'

Roscoe dragged himself upright. The intervention had come none too soon. Not only was blood rippling down from head wounds but it was soaking through his jacket from gashes on his arms.

'You got to help me—'

'Who is this man?'

'Get me to a sodding doctor!'

'Just as soon as you answer my question.'

Dashing the blood from his eyes, Roscoe stood wavering for a second. Dutt thought he'd never seen a more ghastly-looking figure. Then the bookmaker spat with all his remaining strength, spat at Pershore, spat at the policemen.

'He's Palmer if you want to know . . . the joker what took the City and Western Bank!'

And before Gently could catch him he collapsed on the bloodied grass.

CHAPTER SIXTEEN

So, IN EFFECT, it was only the beginning of a case: a case which sent the Fraud Squad delving back twenty-five years. By the time they had finished their reports covered several hundred typewritten sheets, with no prospect whatever of a conviction at the end of it.

But a portrait emerged from their onerous labour, a portrait somehow pathetic as well as sinister. George William Palmer, alias Geoffrey Wallace Pershore, seemed a character belonging to another era.

He was the son of a chauffeur in a small town in Somerset, they had elicited that through Somerset House. By an odd coincidence he had been born on 18th February, 1902; the coincidence being that on that day Thomas Peterson Goudie, whose practices on the Bank of Liverpool might have furnished Palmer with a blueprint, was brought to trial in the Central Criminal Court.

His mother died when he was five. His father – could this have been quite irrelevant? – was in the employ of a rich glove-manufacturer who was a leading citizen and had been mayor of the town in 1909. When Palmer was ten his father was sacked, apparently unjustly, though the chauffeur had immediately got another situation with the widow of a coal-merchant. With her assistance, Palmer was sent to the local grammar school, and by her good graces he was received into the employ of the City and Western Bank at Bristol when his schooldays were ended.

There, for ten years, he was a model employee.

'He was punctual and efficient' – so ran a statement – 'and thoroughly reliable in all his duties. He had a somewhat negative character and appeared to be rather lonely. He seemed to lack initiative and personal ambition.'

Are bank managers among the world's keenest observers?

'Blimey, I knew Palmer!' – this was from another source. 'Always saw him at Bath and the meetings round that way. Quiet sort of a cove, though he dressed up to the nines. Many's the fiver I've took off him on a sure thing what come unstuck.'

And from a respectable publican's wife with five grown-up children: 'He was always such a toff . . . that was before I met Albert, mind you!'

So there had been two sides to Palmer in those distant days. There was the official face, so to speak, and the racecourse dandy. And like Goudie before him, he found that one did not adequately support the other, and like Goudie again, it occurred to him that certain loopholes existed . . .

'The earliest discrepancy occurs on 23rd May, 1930. A cheque debited to Henry Askew, of the Bristol shipowning company, is shown as cleared in the A-D clearance book. The journal is ticked to indicate that the account was posted, but in fact it was never entered in the ledger nor the cheque filed.'

It was Goudie all over again, using the tried and trusted method. Askew, the shipping magnate, had taken the place of Hudson, the soap millionaire. At the weekly audit a Mr Brownlow was shown to be a hundred pounds below his real wealth, but the matter was generously readjusted on the next day after . . .

'For nine months there is no record of further discrepancies.'

This was where Goudie and Palmer parted company. Racing dominated the Scot and drove him from indiscretion to indiscretion, but Palmer, once out of his jam, took care never to get into another one. Quite other ideas had been occurring to the chauffeur's son . . . from now on, he was going to be nobody's mug!

'On 15th March, 1931 a cheque drawn for two thousand pounds in favour of a "D. S. Lane" is shown as cleared and posted, but was not entered in the ledger or filed.'

How that same D. S. Lane was going to bedevil the Fraud Squad investigators through acres of dusty banksheets!

'On 30th March a similar sum, and thereafter until the end of the financial year in April 1932 . . .'

Palmer's procedure was simple. It followed the classic

line at all points. His current account with the bank supplied him with their cheques, and as the A–D ledger clerk he was painfully familiar with Askew's signature. Then, when the forged cheques came back, they disappeared conveniently down the staff WC . . .

'By 10th June, 1934 there was a deficit of exactly two hundred and fifty thousand pounds.'

The danger was, as with Goudie, that some accident might involve the journal and the ledger being compared; but once more fortune seemed to be favouring the bold. As for the audits, they could be got round, though the procedure was growing increasingly complex.

'From that date until his resignation took effect in August Palmer seems to have ceased his operations.'

Always a tidy man, he had wound up his scheme on arriving at a round figure.

'The interval appears to have been spent in the manipulations of his assets, which were dispersed in a number of accounts at various banks. These we believe to have been redeposited, probably in London, but a very full enquiry has failed to elicit . . .'

Palmer, in fact, had successfully covered his tracks, and it remained for him gracefully to disappear from Bristol. His resignation was accepted. He was given excellent references. On 17th August, 1934 he departed on the London express, having just, and for the last time, carried his accounts through the weekly audit.

Six days later the storm broke.

And Palmer, with a quarter of a million pounds, had vanished into the blue.

At that time a sergeant and only recently attached to the Yard, Gently could remember the excitement and clamour of those humid August days. A friend of his, Tebbut, belonged to the Fraud Squad, and he recalled the young man's enthusiasm slowly evaporating into depression – coupled, perhaps, with some grudging admiration for Palmer's magnificent effrontery. At first they were going to get him inside the week – nobody got away with that sort of thing! Then, possibly, it would take a little longer, since by that time it was obvious that chummy had got abroad . . .

And now, finally, twenty-odd years after, it was Gently who was going to fill up the picture . . . the picture of a Palmer suffering a sea-change in Africa, and turning up, as Pershore, to become a leading citizen in another small town.

Had he really been surprised, once, that Pershore drove the Bentley himself?

'I suppose he felt at home here.'

Superintendent Press wanted to talk endlessly about the case. He kept ordering cups of coffee and having to make journeys down the corridor. Each time he came back quickly, as though fearing that Gently would have taken the opportunity to escape.

'Do you know the place he came from? Is it anything like Lynton?'

Oddly enough, it wasn't, except . . .

'There's a similar sort of atmosphere. You get it in all places of about the same size.'

'Ah, that accounts for it!'

'That, and the fact that Lynton is the width of England away from Bristol, and rather cut off.'

'It was a risk, though, wasn't it?'

'Not as much as you might think.'

'But going racing – what about that?'

'I understand he didn't start again until after the war, by which time, being so well secured . . .'

Even so, ten years had elapsed before that fatal day at Newmarket. Nobody who had once known the showy bank clerk had happened on, or recognized, the distinguished frequenter of Tattersall's with his horsey wife and gleaming Bentley. Until a little Stepney spiv with a memory sharpened by malpractice . . .

'He sees him first by the paddock.' Roscoe had joined Blacker in a desire to provide Queen's Evidence. '"Here," he says, "that geezer's dial strikes me as familiar. Now where was it I see *him* before?"'

He hadn't remembered at once – it had been many a long year! – but during the course of the day he probed back into his memory. Twice more they had seen Pershore, the second time as he was leaving, and it was then that the spark of recognition fell.

'Cor blimey O'Riley!'

Taylor had been thunderstruck by his discovery. Could it really be . . . after all this time . . . flourishing on his ill-gotten wealth . . . ?

'Ask any of them what had to do with Steinie – he never forgot the face of a client. Got a gift that way, he had, it was what made him so useful. If Steinie recognized a bloke that was good enough for Jimmy Roscoe.'

A few inquiries amongst the fraternity gave them the name by which Palmer was known. Armed with this, they obtained his address from the nearest telephone directory – phoning, at the same time, for reservations at the Lynton Roebuck.

'I wrote the letter – no names, of course! We made it five thou the first go, just to see how the charlie took it. He came up with it like a bird, no bother at all. Steinie collected it from the convenience near the docks.'

So then, naturally, they doubled it, and after Steinie had been strangled—

'The sky was the flipping limit, and who the hell could blame us?'

As with morality, in turpitude there were degrees.

'The C.C. got a cable from his wife. Tomorrow night she's flying back.'

'Has she money of her own?'

'I believe so, fortunately.'

'It's an interesting point, but with the devaluation since 1934 . . .'

'It wouldn't surprise me if they found his assets . . .'

At last the super seemed to have talked himself out of the subject. For a long time he sat silently staring into his current coffee cup, which was empty. Then, as Gently made signs of rising:

'Do you think he'll hang, or is it genuine?'

Gently's shoulders lifted in his familiar gesture.

' "Regression" they'll call it . . . it's up to the judge. If he sums up against him nine juries out of ten . . .'

'But in your opinion?'

'I'm only a policeman.'

'Nevertheless . . .'

'Do sane people kill?'

The spring weather was probably a flash in the pan, but nobody in Lynton was troubling his head about that. Sports shirts and summer dresses had come out in earnest, and in the Abbey Gardens people were sitting on the grass to eat their sandwiches.

Gently, waiting for the fast train, had been mooching about the town doing nothing in particular. Now he was gazing in a tobacconist's window, now, though he had had his lunch, at the pies in a pork butcher's.

If one was there long enough, did one grow to like Lynton? He hadn't formulated the question, but that was what was passing through his mind. Certainly the place had grown on him, little by little; the streets no longer seemed petty and so depressingly parochial.

Was it the sun, cutting shadows and making the pigeons sleek their feathers?

But he remembered the rain, and before that, the east wind! – he had seen the worst of Lynton and been miserable and out of sorts in it. At one time he had loathed it, as one only loathes a place with which one is out of sympathy.

Yet now, about to leave it . . .

Had he come to understand the place?

'Don't buy that muck – try some of mine!'

He turned to find Blythely, of all people, standing just behind him. He was wearing his black shapeless suit and a cheap tie dragged out of shape – no concession, obviously, to the rising thermometer.

'You don't know what they put in them – a bit of horse, it wouldn't surprise me. Mine are solid pork and a proper piece of pastry round it.'

'I wasn't thinking of buying any . . .'

'I've been in touch with the bank.'

He made an awkward motion as though for Gently to accompany him, and without giving it a thought the man from the Central Office fell into step. Side by side, they made their way along the chequered pavements in the direction of Fenway Road.

'It'll be a takeover, won't it?'

'Undoubtedly the bank will have a major voice.'

'I've put in an offer for it, lock, stock and barrel. I know what it's worth down to the last farthing.'

'You mean the bakehouse?'

'No, the whole lot.'

What was the point of being surprised by anything Blythely did? To begin with, you wouldn't have thought he had a penny with which to bless himself. And then again, looking at that porous, sallow face . . .

'What about Fuller?'

'He hasn't got the money.'

'You'll turn him out?'

'Why? He's a tradesman.'

'I was simply thinking . . .'

Surely Blythely must understand! Already it was bad enough while he was the miller's subtenant – reverse the situation, and the thing became impossible.

Blythely, expressionless as always, was apparently refusing to see it.

'He came to have a talk with me – I don't know what it was all about!'

They were going round by Cosford Street, a way slightly longer than that by the Gardens and The Roebuck.

'He'd got something worrying him, but I couldn't get it clear. I told him to pray if he was in trouble. I doubt whether he did, but Godly advice is never wasted – his conscience seemed clearer after we had spoken together.'

The baker glanced sidelong at Gently as though to canvass his views. They had turned the corner near the crossroads and were approaching the passage to the drying-ground.

'They tell me you're a fisherman.'

Was there no fathoming the man?

'If you want to know where to get some bream, just listen to what I say. A couple of hundred yards below the sluice – the one where they pulled the body out . . .

'Get some groundbait from the mill and use a number twelve hook with a French float. Paste, mind you – I'll give you a special loaf – and if you don't pull a couple of stone out you can't call yourself a fisherman.

'On a good feeding day I've had four or five.'

'Why not come along and show me?'

Gently halted at the top of the passage.

'In the season we could make a day of it – I could give you a ring in advance.'

'As a rule I fish alone . . .'

For once the baker was hesitant. To cover his indecision he pulled out his gold half-hunter and pretended to consult it.

'I don't know but what for once in a while . . .'

'And while we're at it, why not ask Fuller?'

Blythely's foxy eyes jumped suddenly from the watch to Gently. For a long, long moment he seemed unable to drag them away.

'Hmn – I'll have to think about it . . . did you say you'd ring me?'

Gently nodded woodenly. It was his turn to lack expression.